Rocco let out a heavy sigh, looking down at the paperweight on his desk. Straightening it before looking at Charity again. "I find myself growing more impatient. Either get on your knees for me or get out."

"There are no circumstances on earth that would find me on my knees for you. Not begging you, not pleasuring you. That is my firm promise."

Anger cut through his veins like a knife. "We will see about that, or do you forget that I hold your future in my hands?"

She crossed her arms beneath her breasts and tilted her head to the side, that ridiculous ponytail tilting with her, glossy dark curls sweeping over her shoulders. "Before you start making threats, you should know that I carry *your* future in my womb."

One Night With Consequences

When one night...leads to pregnancy!

When succumbing to a night of unbridled desire,
it's impossible to think past the morning after!

But with the sheets barely settled,
the little blue line appears on the pregnancy test
and it doesn't take long to realize that
one night of white-hot passion has turned into
a lifetime of consequences!

Only one question remains:

How do you tell a man you've just met that you're
about to share more than just his bed?

Find out in

Nine Months to Redeem Him by Jennie Lucas
January 2015

Prince Nadir's Secret Heir by Michelle Conder
March 2015

Carrying the Greek's Heir by Sharon Kendrick
April 2015

Married for Amari's Heir by Maisey Yates
July 2015

Bound by the Billionaire's Baby by Cathy Williams
July 2015

More stories in the One Night With Consequences
series can be found at Harlequin.com.

Maisey Yates

Married for Amari's Heir

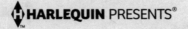

HARLEQUIN PRESENTS®

ISBN-13: 978-0-373-13352-9

Married for Amari's Heir

First North American publication 2015

Copyright © 2015 by Maisey Yates

Recycling programs for this product may not exist in your area.

Printed in U.S.A.

Maisey Yates is a *USA TODAY* bestselling author of more than thirty romance novels. She has a coffee habit she has no interest in kicking, and a slight Pinterest addiction. She lives with her husband and children in the Pacific Northwest. When Maisey isn't writing she can be found singing in the grocery store, shopping for shoes online and probably not doing dishes. Check out her website, maiseyyates.com.

Books by Maisey Yates

Harlequin Presents

His Diamond of Convenience
To Defy a Sheikh
One Night to Risk It All
Forged in the Desert Heat
His Ring Is Not Enough
The Couple Who Fooled the World
A Game of Vows

The Chatsfield
Sheikh's Desert Duty

The Call of Duty
A Royal World Apart
At His Majesty's Request
Pretender to the Throne

Secret Heirs of Powerful Men
Heir to a Desert Legacy
Heir to a Dark Inheritance

The Santina Crown
Princess from the Shadows

Visit the Author Profile page
at Harlequin.com for more titles.

To Limecello, for sharing the picture on Twitter
that sparked the idea for this story.
And for knowing I needed to see it!

CHAPTER ONE

You will meet me at The Mark at 1:30 p.m. You will wear the dress that was sent this afternoon. In this bag is the lingerie you will wear beneath the dress. This is nonnegotiable. If you do not comply, I will know. And you will be punished for it.
—R

CHARITY WYATT LOOKED at the very high-end shopping bag that was sitting on the hall table in her entryway. It was a deep gray color, innocuous, except for the famous lingerie label printed on the side. It had matching slate tissue paper inside, and underneath the very first fold of paper was a thick white envelope with a card inside. She knew, because she had opened it. Opened it and read the instructions that were printed on it while her cheeks burned with rage.

The card was now tucked safely back into the bag. She didn't want to read it again. Once was enough.

The Mark. A clever location to ask for a meet up, since, six months ago, that was what *he* had been to her father. And to her.

A mark, part of a con. A mark who now had her utterly and completely at his mercy. She hated that. Hated being on the losing end. Hated being at a disadvantage.

She should have sent her dad packing when, after nearly a year of no contact, he'd breezed back into her life.

One more, Charity. Just one more.

Just one more and it would all be golden in the end. How many times had she heard that? Always with his signature wink and smile, the charm that got him everywhere in life. Oh, how she'd craved the chance to be in his circle. To be a part of him. To be valuable enough to him that he would take her everywhere. No more time spent on her grandmother's couch, wondering when her dad would be back. No more terrifying nights alone in an empty apartment while he went out and "worked."

It would all end, once he had the perfect score.

He was so good at spinning golden stories out of straw. And she wanted to walk down into the glittering world he always spoke of. Where things were easy. Where they would be together.

But it always took just one more job.

All her life, her dad had promised there would be rainbows after the storms. So far all she'd ever seen was the thunder and lightning. She had yet to get her rainbow, and this time was no exception.

In this instance, he had left her standing in a puddle, holding a lightning rod.

The minute her father had left town she'd known she was up a creek. But she'd stayed. Because she didn't have anywhere else to go. Because she had a life here. Had some friends. Had a job. And she'd been certain she would avoid detection. She always had.

Six months of silence. Six months of her life going on as it always had. Six months to get over her father's betrayal. Six months for her to forget that she had made a powerful enemy.

And now this.

This demand.

It came one day after he'd made contact for the first time. A call to her cell phone from an untraceable number.

She knew what he looked like. Rocco Amari was famous, the media's favorite businessman playboy. He had model good looks, shiny cars, shinier girlfriends. Basically, everything you needed to capture the attention of the public.

She had seen him before in print images, but she had never heard his voice. Until yesterday. Until he'd made contact. She'd realized quickly that she couldn't outrun him, that she couldn't hide from him.

Not without pulling up stakes and disappearing into the night. Leaving her little apartment, her restaurant job, her small group of friends. Becoming a vapor, as she'd been in her childhood. Invisible. With few enough things to stuff them all into one bag so she and her dad could run quickly if they needed to. Then her dad could drop her at his mother's for "a while" at a moment's notice.

No. She hadn't been able to face becoming that person again. A ghost in the human world, never allowed to touch anything. Never allowed to be a part of anything.

So she'd stayed.

Which meant pulling a much more brazen con than she would like. One that would hopefully end this thing with him, and see her on her way. Free and clear. She had to go to him, convince him of her innocence.

But he hadn't been playing by her rules. And then he'd finally called.

"Charity Wyatt?"

"Yes?"

"We've never spoken before, but you know who I am. Rocco, Rocco Amari. You have something that belongs to me, my pretty little thief." His voice was deep, his Italian

*heritage evident in each syllable. It was the kind of voice
that seemed to have a flavor all its own, something smoky,
like Scotch and cigars. It curled itself around her, around
her throat, made it difficult for her to speak.*

"I am not a thief," she said, injecting a note of ringing
conviction into her voice. "My father is a con man and he—"

"And you are his accomplice," he said, the certainty
in his voice squashing the false ring of conviction in hers.

"I need to explain. He lied to me. I didn't know what
I was doing!"

"Yes, yes. Very nice, hysterical cries about your innocence. However, I find myself unmoved."

*She bit her lip, trying to force herself to feel persecuted,
to call up everything she'd felt when her father had left. So
that he could hear a truth that wasn't there.* "But I didn't
mean to steal anything from you."

"And yet, I find myself short a million dollars. And your
father is nowhere to be found. Things must be made right."

"If I could get hold of my father, I would see that he
returned the money." *Even though she knew it had been
put into other assets by now.*

"But you can't get hold of your father, can you?"

*No. No she couldn't. Even if she could, she doubted
he'd be on hand to bail her out of trouble by putting his
own neck on the chopping block. He'd left her to deal with
this on purpose.*

"However," Rocco continued, "I find that I have a sug-
gestion for you...a deal."

"A deal?"

"Yes, but I do not discuss important business on the
phone. You will receive instructions tomorrow. Follow
them, or I will change my mind. And I will press charges.
And you, Ms. Wyatt, will spend quite a few years in jail
for fraud and theft."

* * *

And that was how she found herself here. With these instructions, with this bag, with the dress that was still sitting in its garment bag, because she was afraid to look at it.

But then, ignoring it wouldn't make it go away. Ignoring Rocco wouldn't make him go away. Wouldn't remove the threat that had been placed on her freedom.

She would have to go to the meeting. She would have to comply with his instructions.

And after that, she had no idea what she would do. Her eyes fell to the lingerie bag again. A shiver of disgust wound down her spine. She didn't know what his offer would be, but a suspicion was starting to form. One that didn't sit well at all. One that, now it had entered her mind, would not be removed.

It was silly, of course, because she couldn't imagine why he would want *her* in lieu of a million dollars or justice. But there was lingerie. That fact remained.

No matter what her concerns, she had no choice but to comply.

It was either that or jail.

And as terrifying as the bag of lingerie was, an orange jumpsuit was far, far scarier. There were enough courtroom dramas on TV painting law and order as a great equalizer that Charity knew most people must see the justice system as something that protected them.

She never had.

Her father had talked about Robin Hood. Twisting tales where thieves were heroes and anyone in uniform was out to shore up the impossible walls built around the rich and elite. Walls that kept people like them down and out.

Yes. The law was nothing but evil. Jail, the worst fate that could befall someone like them because they could disappear in there. No one on the outside cared about people like them. The ones on the bottom rung of society. They had to take care of themselves, because no one else would.

There was a very large part of her that still clung to those teachings, was still shaped by them.

But she'd talked her way out of worse.

She just had to find her angle.

And once she found it, she would exploit it to the best of her ability. And her abilities on that score were pretty damn good.

Rocco might think he had the upper hand…and she would allow him to continue thinking that.

The dress was so tight that Charity could barely breathe. Sheer layers of black lace that clung to her curves and revealed hints of skin beneath. There had been shoes in the bag which, somehow, fit her, just like the dress. Just like the lingerie. The heels were tall, and given the brief hemline of the garment, lengthened her legs and showed a whole lot more skin than she was comfortable with.

Which was, in many ways, going to work to her advantage. The fact that she was uncomfortable in these clothes would help. She could use it, and use them.

Charity took a deep breath and walked through the black entryway doors of The Mark, her impractical heels clicking loudly on the black-and-white-striped tile. She walked through the lobby area into the entrance of the restaurant, feeling her face heat when the hostess appraised her.

The woman's expression remained neutral, and yet, somehow, Charity sensed a hint of disdain beneath it.

She could well imagine that women in tight, tiny dresses only served one purpose in an establishment like this. If Rocco had intended to humiliate her, he was doing a very fine job.

Yet again, not necessarily a bad thing. Because she could embrace that. Go ahead and welcome the heat she could feel spreading in her face, the slight trembling in her legs. All the better to play the part of shivering ingénue.

All the better to appeal to his humanity.

"I'm here to see…Rocco Amari," she said, placing a slight hesitation before his name. Getting into character already.

This earned her a slight smile. "Of course, miss. Mr. Amari keeps his own private table in the back of the dining room. He has not arrived yet, but I'm happy to show you to your seat."

The hostess turned and began to walk into the dining room, and Charity followed. Her high heels sank into the plush carpet, her ankle rolling slightly with each step. She put all of her focus on walking in a straight line and not breaking a bone.

She hadn't worn shoes like this in a while. The mangled sidewalks that ran through the ancient New York neighborhood she lived in certainly weren't practical for this kind of footwear. And in her line of work, she rarely wore anything fancier than black slacks and a black polo shirt. Along with some very sensible sneakers that allowed her to stand on her feet all day.

Her waitressing job, at a restaurant that was much less posh than this one, was the first real job she'd ever had. After her dad had left last year she'd wanted to get out of their "family business." She was old enough now to understand that running cons wasn't just a job, and that, no matter how rich or terrible the people you conned were, it wasn't any way to live your life in the long term.

But then he'd come back, all beguiling smiles and laughter, the kind she'd missed since he'd been gone, and he'd asked her to help him again.

Just one more time...

She could stab her own arm with the salad fork. She was such an idiot. She was a con who'd been conned by a con. And now she was in too deep.

"Can I get you anything to drink?" the hostess asked.

Charity weighed her options. On the one hand, sobriety would definitely be an asset when dealing with a man like Rocco. On the other hand, she needed something to help her get a handle on her nerves. Sometimes wine made conversation flow a little more smoothly.

"White wine," she said. She didn't have to drink it after all. But it would be there if she needed it.

"Of course, miss." The hostess disappeared, leaving Charity sitting alone.

Charity glanced at the menu, not really bothering to read the descriptions of the food. Everything would be good at a place like this, but she was feeling a little nervous. Her stomach always got funny when she was lying. Which was inconvenient when you had to lie a lot.

While she was skimming the menu a hush fell over the restaurant. Or, perhaps the restaurant had already been hushed and something else in the atmosphere changed. Grew thicker, tighter.

Whatever it was, there was a change.

She looked up, just in time to see a man walk in. He was arresting, and she wasn't the only one who found him so. It seemed that almost every eye in the restaurant—male and female—was on him. He was tall, sleek like a panther. His black hair slicked back off his forehead, trim physique encased in a black suit that was tailored perfectly to the stark, lean lines of his body. But it wasn't his clothing, or the handmade Italian shoes on his feet, nor the impossibly expensive gold watch on his wrist and the no doubt overpriced sunglasses he pulled from over his eyes as he walked deeper into the restaurant, that held everyone's attention.

It was something deeper. Something more. A magnetism that could not be denied.

Everything about him was designed to capture and hold the attention of an audience.

And as he drew closer she could see that he was extraordinarily handsome. Olive skin, high cheekbones, a strong, straight nose. And his lips… She couldn't remember ever noticing a man's lips before, but she certainly noticed his.

Rocco Amari was even more beautiful in person than he was in the glossy pages of a magazine. So annoying. Why couldn't he be a sad disappointment?

"Ms. Wyatt," he said, that voice as affecting now as it had been over the phone. "I am pleased to see you made it. And that you found the dress to your liking."

That comment made her wish her wine was already here, so she could throw it in his face. He had given her no choice, and he knew it.

Don't let him get to you. You have to get to him.

"It is a very good fit," she said. "As we have never met before, I was a little bit surprised by that."

"Oh, I had you investigated. Very thoroughly." He took a seat in the chair opposite her, undoing the button on his jacket as he did, and suddenly several members of staff seemed to materialize out of nowhere. "We will have what the chef recommends," he said.

The staff melted into obscurity after that and Rocco turned his full attention to her, his dark eyes blazing with a kind of sharpness that seemed to cut through her. It was disconcerting to say the least.

A new waitress, one she had not seen before, set her white wine down in front of her. Charity grasped the stem, needing something to keep her hands busy.

"Hopefully that pairs well with the meal," he said, looking pointedly at her drink.

"I will say, that is not my primary concern at this point."

"It is always a primary concern of mine. I appreciate life's luxuries. Good food paired with good wine, good Scotch and beautiful women. Which, I must say, Ms. Wyatt, you are." He practically purred the last bit of his sentence, the roughness in the words rippling over her skin, making her break out in goose bumps.

What was wrong with her? She didn't play this game. Didn't go for flirtations and teases. She always had to keep her wits sharp, and that meant no melting around sexy men.

"I suppose I should say thank you, but I'm not going to. Because I feel like you're only putting off the inevitable conversation we must have."

"Perhaps I am," he said. "They serve very good food here. I should hate to spoil the meal."

Charity looked to the left and noticed a table full of upscale Manhattanite women staring at them. Likely wondering what a woman like Charity was doing with a man like Rocco. Just as those women read upper class from their perfectly coiffed hair down to the tips of their designer shoes, Charity read low-class pretender. Even a couture dress couldn't fix that. She had all the hallmarks of a woman who was here on her dining partner's dime.

She knew these things because her father had made a study of the upper class. Had learned their every mannerism, in order to inveigle his way into their midst. All the better to steal their money.

Charity hadn't spent much time playing those parts. Especially when she'd been young, her function in her father's schemes had been to play the part of wide-eyed ragamuffin. A downtrodden innocent who desperately needed help.

It was the role she would be reprising tonight. And while she wouldn't thank her dad for abandoning her to face the music alone, she would thank him, albeit silently, for giving her the tools to fix the broken mess he'd left.

"The meal was spoiled for me before I came," she said, injecting a healthy bit of conviction into her tone.

Rocco didn't seem moved by it. He extended his hand, brushing her cheekbone with the back of his knuckles. She was so shocked, all she could do was sit frozen, a flash of heat radiating from her cheek downward. She looked at the table of women again, saw their sneers and looked down at her wine.

Of course they assumed she was a call girl. Sitting there in that dress in the afternoon. Either a call girl or a kept woman, although there were few differences. They thought they were better than her. Because they were born with what she couldn't even earn.

But she was used to that.

"Come now. I do not want a difficult lunch partner."

"You knew people would think this," she said, her voice low, vibrating with manufactured emotion. "You knew they would think I was your...whore." She made sure to meet his gaze. "I'm not that kind of girl."

She nearly cringed at that overbaked line. But she was having a very easy time accessing this justified rage. *She* almost believed that she was nothing more than a wronged innocent. Almost.

He moved his hand back to her, and caught her chin with his thumb and forefinger, holding her face steady. And suddenly all her false anger was forgotten. "But, *cara mia*, that is what you are. You are here because I have offered you something. You are here because I've offered you a deal. And, do not forget, I bought everything you are wearing."

He was a horror. Nothing seemed to shake him up. He was heartless. Which might be problematic.

She jerked out of his hold, and he lowered his hand. "Just tell me what you want."

The waitstaff appeared again, placing food in front of them, and Charity's stomach turned. She needed this to be over, soon. The longer this stretched out, the less likely he was to bend.

Rocco had no such issues with the meal. He ate slowly, in silence, relishing each bite. The minute stretching out longer, every second a torture. She didn't want to say too much, and she really didn't want to say too little. He seemed fine sitting in silence, letting her feeling of being a mouse caught in a trap intensify beneath the study of his dark gaze.

Worse, the longer he looked at her, the more acutely aware she became of the feeling of the soft, expensive lingerie that was beneath her dress. It was something about the way he looked at her. The fact that he *knew*.

She could see it in his eyes. That he knew exactly what she was wearing, and that he knew what she might look like in the items he had sent.

He was looking at her as if she was a possession, as if he owned her already.

And the fact was, he might. The longer she sat there, the longer she'd had to fully understand her potential fate and the circumstances she found herself in. She didn't know what he would demand of her yet. But she knew the alternative.

Yet another thing he had accomplished by bringing her here. He highlighted the difference in their stations.

She was a waitress; she was a woman. Her ties to criminal activity were irrefutable, though she had never once been arrested. Her father was gone with the money he had taken from Amari Corporation, and he likely wouldn't resurface even if Charity were brought to trial. Actually, if Charity were brought to trial he would be less likely to surface than ever. Because Nolan Wyatt would not stick his neck on the chopping block for anyone. Not even his only daughter. Not when it was between a life of luxury—albeit a temporary one—or life in prison.

Charity would be made the example. She would be brought to court, a scarlet woman who had stolen from a man who worked hard for his money. And she would go to jail. She could see it playing out now.

But he was prepared to offer her a deal. One that would mean avoiding jail.

Realistically, she wasn't sure she could turn it down no matter what it was.

Even if it was the worst.

In that moment she hated herself for being such a coward. For entertaining the idea of selling herself in exchange for avoiding time spent in prison. But she was afraid. Jail was the big bad. Growing up, the law had been a terrifying prospect, men in uniform the enemy.

It was a fear that was bred so deeply into her that just thinking about it now made her break out into a cold sweat. She was afraid of the unknown, and while both options she was entertaining in her mind were unknown, one would be over much faster.

You don't know that's what he wants.

No, she didn't know. But he had sent lingerie, and that said an awful lot.

And she wasn't naive about men. Her father was a liar and a manipulator. And both in word and by example, he'd taught her how to identify other liars and manipulators. Charity wasn't naive about anyone or their motivations.

She liked to be prepared for the worst. And in this case... Well, in this case it meant that Rocco had dressed her for the job he intended her to perform.

Another waiter appeared as soon as Rocco had cleaned his plate. "Dessert, Mr. Amari?"

"No—" the words left Charity's mouth before she could reconsider them "—no dessert."

"Please have dessert and coffee sent to my suite," Rocco said, as though she hadn't spoken. "Ms. Wyatt and I are ready to retire."

"Of course, sir." The waiter inclined his head, his bland expression not betraying any thought whatsoever, and scurried away to do Mr. Amari's bidding.

Charity's stomach sank to her toes, a sick feeling overtaking her. He wanted to take her somewhere private. He wanted to get her alone. Nothing good would come of that. "Are we going to discuss the deal?" She didn't want to leave the dining room. She needed him to change his mind here.

"Of course. Up in my room. And this is the part where I will discover if you heeded my warning."

Her heartbeat sped up, her pulse beating rapidly at the base of her neck. "What warning?" she asked, her throat dry. Because she knew which warning. She *knew*.

"If you are not wearing the lingerie I sent, I am about to find out."

"I haven't agreed to anything," she said, her eyes meeting his. She tried to remind herself to dial it back. To appeal to him on an emotional level.

Challenging a man like him wouldn't get her anywhere. He was all alpha male. If she tried to go at him head-on, he would push back. But if she played the weak, simpering female, she might just be able to arouse his protective instincts. She had to remember that. She had to stay in character.

"You will agree to whatever I ask. Because if we go to court, I will win. You know that to be true."

She swallowed hard, not bothering to disguise it. She wanted him to see her every nerve. Every flicker of fear in her eyes. Being brave wouldn't win any points with him. "I don't understand how this would benefit you."

"But you see, *cara*, that is not for you to understand. I do not have to explain myself to you. I merely have to present you with your options." He put his hands on the table, his large fingers splayed over the pristine white cloth. "So you tell me, would you rather come to my suite or go to jail?"

Charity looked down at her untouched lunch, her lips cold. "If those are my options I would rather go to your suite," she said, determination washing through her like a tide.

She could still turn this around. She would make him see that she was just a victim. She repeated the mantra over and over again. If she said it enough times, she might believe it. And if she believed it…all the better to make him believe it, too.

"Very good." Rocco stood and walked toward her, extending a hand as though he were the perfect gentleman seeing to his companion. She didn't accept the hand, standing up on her own, taking the hard glitter in his eyes as a personal triumph.

"I very much appreciate a strong-willed woman. But I also require compliance when it is demanded." He straightened his cuffs, buttoned his jacket, then raised his focus to her, his dark gaze locking on to her. "I hope very much that you have given it where I have commanded. Otherwise, you will find my threats are not empty." He held out his hand, and this time she took it. "Now, come, *cara mia*. It is time for us to adjourn to my room."

CHAPTER TWO

THE SUITE WAS BEAUTIFUL. There were massive windows that overlooked Central Park, letting a generous amount of natural light in, bathing everything in warmth, in sunlight. For a moment, she simply stood in the doorway, pretending she was only taking in the sight of a beautiful room. One that was well out of her price range, one she would typically never even get to look at.

Unless she was running a con.

That's all this is. You're just running a con. And on the other side, lies freedom. You never have to do it again. You can be done.

She took a deep breath and kept examining the room, delaying the moment this became real. The floors were marble, rugs stationed throughout, beautifully appointed matching furniture with solid wood detail in the seating area, with a bed that boasted a matching frame in the bedroom. It was a large bed, with rich purple velvet coverings, and more pillows than she had ever seen in one place before.

For a moment, it was nice to look at. For a moment, it seemed innocuous.

But only for a moment.

Then Rocco came to stand behind her, the heat from his body intense, energy radiating from him and throwing everything inside of her out of alignment. As if he'd reached into her chest and moved everything around.

He had certainly reached into her life and done that. Moved everything around, put things on their ends.

"Dessert should be here shortly," he said, breezing past her and walking into the room. "Make yourself at home."

As if that was going to happen. "It's difficult for me to feel at home here."

"Oh yes, I imagine it is quite different to your little apartment in Brooklyn."

Charity froze. Of course he would know all about her. He had sent the clothes to her home, after all. But hearing the details of her life spoken about by a perfect stranger just didn't sit comfortably.

"Do you have to imagine?" she asked, her tone crisp. "Don't you happen to have full walk-through photographs of my home available for your perusal? You seem to know a lot about me."

"The art of war. One must know their enemies. Or so I have read."

"And I'm your enemy?"

He closed the distance between them, curling his fingers around her arm, pulling her close. The contact of his skin against hers struck her like lightning. "You stole from me. People do not steal from me," he said, his face close to hers, his tone deadly.

She could sense then that he was every inch the predator she had feared. And whatever she had been afraid he might ask of her, it would likely be that and more. Because there was no softness in him. No compassion.

He was the sort of man who only understood one thing. The cutthroat, black-and-white nature of revenge. Of killing or being killed, hunting or being hunted.

That would limit her ability to manipulate. But her strength would lie in him underestimating her.

He thought she was his prey. But he didn't know that beneath this lacy monstrosity beat the heart of a beast. She had been brought up in a hard environment, with instability and poverty and all the rest.

She hadn't survived by being weak.

"My father lied to me," she said, putting her hand on her chest, feeling her heart beating hard beneath her palm. "I really thought he had finally gotten honest work. I had agreed to help him garner investments from reputable companies. I did not know he was going to take that information and siphon money out of your accounts. I promise I didn't know." The lie came easy, even looking into those flat, dark eyes. Because protecting her own skin was second nature. Was the most important thing. The only thing.

"Your name is on the wire transfers. Your name is connected to the bank account the money went into."

"Because I agreed to help him set the accounts up." And she knew, even as she tried to explain, that it was going to do nothing to move him. But she wasn't going to simply stand here and allow him to level accusations at her. Not when they weren't true. Not while she still had a chance to get him to understand.

"Then you are a fool. Because everything I can find about Nolan Wyatt says that he is a con man. Now and always."

"He is," she said, her throat tight. "But I—"

There was a knock on the door to the suite and Rocco released his hold on her, stalking to the entryway.

"Room service, Mr. Amari," the man on the other side of the door said. "Where would you like me to put the tray?"

"I will take the tray." Rocco took control of the tray

and closed the door, wheeling the coffee and two pieces of chocolate cake to the center of the room.

If she couldn't eat a light meal of vegetables and salmon, she was hardly going to be able to eat this.

"Haven't you ever wanted to believe the best of someone?" She hoped he had. She hoped he did.

"Never. I only want the truth."

"I'm giving it to you. And I can only explain away the fact that I helped my father by saying I wanted to believe the best in him when I shouldn't have. He's the only family I have. I just wanted him to be telling the truth this time."

She found herself very convincing. She would be shocked if he didn't.

"So much that you were willing to take a chance on helping him with another fraud?"

"My dad is small-time. I didn't expect anything like this from him." That much was true. She'd had no idea his designs were quite so grand. A million dollars. He'd overplayed his hand. The idiot. Anything smaller and Rocco wouldn't have noticed, much less pursued her like this. "Yes, he's stolen fairly large amounts of money before, and I know it. I didn't live with him most of the time I was growing up, but when I did, we would always have times where we would move, and then we would have something for a while. A house, food, money, clothes. But it would always disappear very quickly. We would find ourselves dodging landlords, dodging police. Then, we would move again. Dad would get *jobs*, he called them. Then we would move again, and have things for a while. And the cycle would repeat. Eventually, he stopped taking me with him when he moved."

"I see. Is this meant to make me feel sorry for you?"

"I only want you to understand…I'm a person like you

are," she said, a pleading note lacing her voice. "I made a mistake in who I trusted. Surely you understand?"

He chuckled, a hollow sound that echoed in her chest. That made goose bumps spread over her arms. "The problem with trying to appeal to my humanity, Charity, is that I don't have any. I can understand why you would assume differently. But let me be the one to inform you definitively that I'm not burdened by conscience. Nor am I burdened by compassion. Every cent I have, I have earned. Getting to this position in life cost me in blood and I will not allow myself to be taken advantage of. I will set an example if I must." He moved to her again, not touching her this time, merely standing so close she could feel the heat coming from his body. "I will make an example of you if I must. Do not think I will lose sleep over throwing a beautiful woman like you in prison when it is deserved."

"So, is this my last meal?" she asked, indicating the food on the tray.

Overdramatic, perhaps, but she was starting to feel desperate.

"Either that or it is fuel to help you keep up your strength for the next couple of hours. You might find you need it."

Adrenaline spiked through her blood. "So, you get off on forcing women into bed?" The words came out slightly harsher than intended.

A smile curved his lips. "Absolutely not. I never force women into my bed. I will not force you. You will come to me, because you want me."

"How would you know I wanted you? When it's you or a jail cell it seems as though my choices are limited."

"I'm comfortable with that," he said, his smile growing wider. He looked like the Big Bad Wolf, ready to devour her. "Would you like some coffee?"

"No."

"Very well. Then it is time for me to see if you have kept your end of the bargain."

She swallowed hard, her hands shaking, her fingers cold. "The lingerie?"

"Did you do as you were instructed, *cara mia*?"

She couldn't believe it. She had lost.

Her stomach sank into her feet, the intense weight of defeat crushing her before she was able to process all the implications in front of her.

This was the moment of truth. Either she threw the coffee on his face and stormed out of the room, and took what came, later—charges, an arrest, a trial.

Or she did this.

She took control. She pushed him as he was pushing her. Called his bluff.

She would not stand here and wait to be undressed.

Before she could think it through, her shaking fingers found the zipper to her dress and began to tug it down.

He would stop her. He would stop this. She was sure of it. And it was that certainty that kept her going.

She could feel the fabric separating, exposing skin. Could feel the dress getting loose in the bodice. Then the top fell exposing her breasts, clad only in the whisper-thin lingerie. It was the same color as her skin, a kind of milky coffee color. It made her appear almost bare.

She knew, because she had spent a fair amount of time looking at herself in the mirror wearing this, that he would be able to see the shadow of her nipples beneath the fabric.

No man had ever seen this much of her body before. She didn't know if she was in shock, if she was still convinced he would put an end to it, or if the moment was simply too surreal for her to absorb it all. But she felt cushioned by something, by a gauzy curtain that had been pulled around her vision, making things seem hazy. Making them seem a little less harsh.

Whatever it was, whatever magic this was, she needed it. Because the character, the nervous ingénue, wasn't a refuge here. Not now.

It was too close to the bone.

Too close to who she was in this setting.

In life, she had very little in the way of innocence. But here? In the bedroom? She'd never trusted a man enough to be this intimate with him. Had never wanted to.

And she didn't trust him. But she didn't need to. For some reason, right now, she realized trust didn't matter. This was all about power. And he had underestimated hers.

She finished pulling the zipper down the rest of the way and pushed the dress down her hips so that she was standing there in nothing but the high heels and the matching bra and panty set. The panties were as sheer as the bra, and she knew he could see the shadow of dark hair at the apex of her thighs.

She stared straight ahead, not looking at him, her eyes fixed on a blank spot on the wall. She was still in this chess game and her new revelation was adjusting her strategy. Putting her in view of Rocco's queen.

Power. Control. That was the game here. It wasn't sex.

All she had to do was take his control.

"Look at me," Rocco said, his voice laced with steel, the command impossible to ignore.

She redirected her gaze, her eyes clashing with his, and all the breath rushed from her lungs.

There was an intensity to his dark gaze that was unmatched by anything she had ever seen before. It could never be said that Rocco looked passive, at least not in her very brief experience of him. But this was different. There was a fire burning beneath this that set something ablaze low and hot inside of her.

He moved toward her, reaching out and touching the silken strap of the bra, sliding his thumb and forefinger over the fabric. "You were a very good girl. I must confess I am surprised." He never took his eyes off hers, and the heat inside of her intensified.

What was happening to her? Why was he touching her? Not her skin, but beneath it? Why was he making her feel all this heat?

She could still leave. She could still pick up her dress, put it back on and go.

But she didn't. Instead she stood, frozen, as fascinated as she was terrified by what might happen next.

He leaned in slowly and she held her breath. He pressed his lips against the curve of her neck, just beneath her ear, and a shiver went through her body.

She wasn't cold at all anymore. But she was still shaking. And it wasn't from fear.

"I will make you beg for me," he said, his voice a dark whisper that wrapped itself around her mind.

She angled her head slightly, pushing down every bit of insecurity. She hated this man. This beautiful, horrible man. And she didn't care what he thought about her. She didn't care what he thought of her body. What he thought of her soul.

He was her enemy and after today she would never see him again.

For some reason that realization sent a shock wave through her. Confidence, pleasure, a rolling feeling of satisfaction that she couldn't have explained if she wanted to.

She leaned in, her lips a breath away from his. "Not if I make you beg for me first."

His lip curled and he leaned in, tracing the line of her

jaw with his forefinger. "Do you think you could make me beg?"

"Can you walk away?" she asked, taking the roughness in his formerly smooth and cultured voice as evidence of the effect she was having on him. "Right now, could you leave this room?"

"I am not finished with you yet," he ground out.

She forced a smile to curve the corner of her mouth. "I guess that says it all. You're the one who can't walk away. And I don't even have prison to threaten you with."

He gripped her chin tight, and she stared him down. His dark eyes were blazing and she was certain hers matched. Then he slid his thumb across the edge of her lower lip.

And closed the distance between them.

The fire in her stomach ignited, sending flames roaring through her. It was no longer contained, no longer content to merely burn in the hearth. And she realized her fatal mistake too late. She might have taken his control, but hers was gone, too. Whatever this heat was had taken over everything, threatening to reduce all that she was to ash.

She'd never been kissed like this. Had never been held close to a man like this, his arms so tight around her, his body hard and muscular against hers.

This was the last thing she had expected. For him to kiss her as if he was a man dying of thirst and she was an oasis. She had expected him to be cool. She had expected him to hurt her, humiliate her. She hadn't expected him to make her want.

Make her feel.

Wanting him was almost scarier than the alternative. Because she was only here for one reason, for him to extract the debt she owed from her body. She meant nothing to him beyond that. In fact, he *hated* her. Saw her as an enemy.

She had a feeling that right at that moment, neither of them had the control. She wasn't even sure if they were fighting for it. If each brush of his lips against hers was a press for more dominance, or if they'd both given up altogether.

She was forgetting. Forgetting everything but his lips against hers.

He shifted, cupped her face, tilting his head and deepening the kiss, his tongue sliding against hers. The delicious friction sent a shiver through her. It shocked her, sent a wave of pleasure through her and, for a moment, she could only process how good it felt.

How could he touch an enemy like this? How could he hate her and taste her so deeply? With such care?

No one else ever had. Only this man. This man who despised her.

That should make her want to run, but she didn't. She stayed. Rooted to the spot. Anchored to him.

When they parted, he was breathing hard, his fingers going to the knot of his tie, loosening it with startling efficiency, before casting into the ground. "Yes, you are a very good girl indeed," he said, his voice ragged.

He pulled her back to him, kissing her again. She wanted to fight him. Wanted to fight this. The way it felt as if he was stripping her bare without ever touching the silken undergarments that covered her skin.

But she couldn't. She felt so small, but she didn't feel weak. She felt protected. And as things started to crumble and fall inside her; as the walls, the anger, the fear, started to crack, in the deep, empty well that lived inside of her, an insatiable and hungry thing that had craved this simply opened up and allowed itself to be filled.

Oh, it hadn't been sex she desired specifically. But touch, attention. To have someone look at her as though she mattered. As though it had to be *her* standing there in front of them and no one else.

To have someone pay attention to what she wanted, what she liked. To have someone lavish pleasure on her. Because that was the only way she could think of it. She was entirely bathed in sensation, the singular focus of this large, powerful man.

He wasn't handling her roughly, not with anger. He was in supreme, complete control and he was exercising that control to make her feel…good.

It wasn't what she had expected and it made her feel vulnerable. Strange.

No one had ever wanted her. No one had ever needed her.

And even if it was naive, she felt in this moment that Rocco *needed* her. And it made her want to give in to him. It made her want to give him everything.

He hates you. And you are trading your body to keep yourself out of jail.

You can't do this.

She could still leave. She could walk out the door and damn the consequences. He wouldn't physically stop her. She was confident in that.

But you don't want to.

No. Because she'd never had the courage to touch a man like this. To kiss a man like this. And now there was nothing holding her back. Nothing stopping her. Why not have this? Why not have him? She pressed her palms to the hard muscle of his chest, and leaned in deeper for the kiss.

Rocco growled, tightening his hold on her waist, and backing them both across the room, and to the bed.

Yes.

This wasn't about money, or jail, or freedom or fear. This wasn't about control. Not now. This was about him.

About everything she'd spent her life too afraid to grab. She was so tired of it. So tired of herself. Of being a ghost that no one could touch or connect with because she was hiding her past.

He was touching her. And he knew her past. He knew it and hated it and he still wanted her. That meant it didn't matter what she did now. Didn't matter that she was a virgin who had no clue what she was doing.

She slid her hands to his shoulders, and down his back, exploring the feel of him, the sheer breadth of him. So different to her. To her body.

He moved one hand to her thigh, lifting her leg and bringing it around his own, opening her center to him. He pressed himself against her, the hard length of his arousal making contact with the source of her desire, sending a shot of pleasure through her body.

It was happening so fast, and yet she found not fast enough. She couldn't think anymore, couldn't reason. Couldn't work out why she had been so afraid of this being the outcome. Because this wasn't scary. And it didn't hurt.

It felt wonderful.

And everything melted away. Who she was. Who he was.

He wasn't a mark. And she wasn't a con artist.

He was a man. And she was a woman.

And *they* wanted.

He tore his mouth from hers, kissing the line along her collarbone, to the edge of the lace bra that she knew had cost more than a month of her wages. He traced the scalloped edge of the delicate garment with the tip of his tongue, and she shook, sliding her fingers through his hair, holding him tightly to her.

"You are delicious," he said, forcing one of the lace cups down, exposing the entirety of her breast to him. Then he lowered his head, taking her nipple into his mouth and sucking deeply. "Delicious," he said, turning his focus to the other breast and repeating the motion.

He slid a thumb over one of the tightened buds, his eyes rapt on her body, watching as it tightened further while he teased her. He pinched her gently and she gasped, arching against him, bringing the heart of her body into contact with his hardness again.

"I did not anticipate wanting you so much," he said. "You are so responsive."

Was she? She wanted to ask him if she was especially responsive, but she couldn't speak. Couldn't do anything but feel.

"Responsive," he said, kissing the valley between her breasts, "and very delicious. I mentioned that, but it must be said again. And I must taste you again." He moved lower, kissing her stomach, and lower still, his lips hovering above the waistband of her panties.

He couldn't mean to…he wouldn't. Because somewhere in the back of her mind she thought that this was a selfless act. One that would mean giving to her, and revenge wasn't selfless. Revenge wouldn't allow him to give that.

But then he was pulling those expensive panties down her legs and forcing her thighs apart, opening her to him. And he looked. More than looked, he stopped, frozen for a moment, and gazed as though she was a work of art in a museum, and he was poring over her every detail.

She could hardly breathe, her heart beating so hard she thought it might burst through her chest.

Then he leaned in, his eyes never leaving hers, his tongue trailing a line along the sensitive skin of her inner thigh. Then he moved close to…to…

A burst of insecurity broke over her. "I don't…you don't have to…"

He growled and pushed his hands beneath her bottom, tugging her close to his mouth, his eyes still on hers. "I will have whatever I like."

He closed the distance between them then, laving the sensitive bundle of nerves with the flat of his tongue. And she stopped pushing at him. Instead, her fingers curled into claws, dug into his skin. For a moment she was afraid she was hurting him, but he let out that low, feral growl again and pulled her more tightly against his mouth, tasting her even deeper, and that thought, along with every other thought she'd ever had, fled from her mind.

She found herself flexing her hips in time with his tongue, pushing herself closer to the edge of climax. She'd never done this with a man before, but she was familiar enough with how her body worked. Though, it was different when someone else had so much of the control. Wilder. More exciting.

He shifted, and she felt his finger slide through her slick flesh, testing the entrance to her body. She tensed, unsure of what to expect next. He pressed into her, the sensation unfamiliar, but not at all painful.

She let out the breath she'd just brought in, and relaxed into the new rhythm, into the feeling of being filled by him. Pleasure started building again, harder, faster. And then it broke over her, a wave that pushed her out to sea, tumbling her in the surf before bringing her up short, spent, and breathless.

She forgot everything. Why she was here. That he was a stranger. That he was her enemy.

How could he be a stranger when he had just touched her more intimately than anyone else ever had? How could he be an enemy when he had taken greater care for her pleasure, her needs and her comfort than anyone else in her life ever had?

And for a moment, just for a moment, he moved up so their bodies were aligned, and he held her in his strong arms, against his solid chest, so that she could rest her head against him and feel the raging of his beating heart, and she felt...she felt home.

Safe.

Cared for.

More for him, more in his arms than she'd ever felt before.

He moved his hand down between her thighs, then leaned in, kissing her neck as he teased her clitoris with his fingers, arousing her again, much more quickly after her orgasm than she would have imagined possible.

She wanted to beg. But somewhere in her mind she remembered him saying she would. And so she bit her lip to hold it back.

Then he lowered his forehead against hers, sweat beading on his skin. She could feel his arousal pressed against her inner thigh, so close. So close to what she knew they both wanted.

"Per favore." He whispered the broken words in Italian, and his need was the final bit of fuel on the flame.

She released her hold on what was left of her control.

"Yes," she said, her voice a sob. "Please. Please take me." She was desperate, and she didn't care if he knew it. And it wasn't just for pleasure, but for a connection. For an answer to the deep, unending emptiness inside her she hadn't been aware of until this moment.

"You want this?" he whispered, the words frayed. "You want me inside you?"

"Yes," she moaned, arching against him.

He kissed her lips before moving away from her, opening the drawer of the nightstand by the bed and producing a little square packet.

A condom.

Oh yes, they weren't done. This was it. She was going to lose her virginity now. To him. And she couldn't even muster any fear. No shame. No doubt. Because she just wanted. More of what he'd given her only moments ago, more of being skin to skin with him. More of his lips against hers, his body *in* hers. She wanted more.

She wanted it all.

He worked the buckle on his dress pants and shoved them partway down his lean hips before positioning himself over her, and tearing open the condom. He was still almost entirely dressed, and she saw nothing but the deft movements of his hand as he rolled the condom over himself.

But when he moved to her entrance, she felt the blunt head of him, stretching her, tearing the thin barrier she'd never before given much thought about. She tensed, squeezing her eyes shut tight as the burning pain reached its peak, then dissipated slowly after he'd buried himself to the hilt.

She gritted her teeth, fought to keep from crying out, but she wasn't successful. A whimper escaped her lips and she shivered beneath him as pain laced its way around all the beautiful pleasure she'd felt only a moment before.

He swore, violent, rough against her ear, and pushed himself up, dark eyes blazing into hers. But he said nothing.

Instead he angled his face and kissed her, long and deep, as he withdrew slowly from her body before sliding back home. It didn't hurt at all that time, and as he established a steady rhythm to his thrusts, discomfort faded to a kind of neutral fullness, and from there grew, expanding to a deep, pulsing pleasure that was unlike anything she'd ever felt before.

She arched against him, as she'd done when he'd gone down on her, meeting his every thrust, the motion sending little sparks of heat through her, a familiar tightness coiling low in her stomach.

She felt him start to shake, felt the control in his movements start to slip. A groan escaped his lips, and he bucked hard against her, freezing above her, pushing them both over the edge to oblivion.

When she came back to herself, she was lying on her back, starting at an unfamiliar ceiling, with his warm, protective weight covering her. As if she was something precious.

Except…he wasn't protective. And she wasn't precious.

She was nothing more than a criminal, who had tried to make good for a while and failed. And he was…he was…

She tried to push away the reality that was crowding in. Tried to ignore the truth she would have to face eventually. She didn't want to. Not now. Not while pleasure was still buzzing through her. Not while she still felt so good.

The power she'd felt only a few moments before was slipping through her grip like sand through an hourglass and there was no way for her to turn it back over and start again.

Then he was up, moving away from her, turning and walking into the bathroom, slamming the door shut behind him.

And she could only lie where she was, still staring at that ceiling. At the way the molding formed different tiers and textures. She listened to the sounds of the streets outside filtering up, audible even through the closed windows.

Life was moving out there, and yet, in here, in this room, in this moment, she was frozen.

The bathroom door opened and Rocco reappeared, his shirt buttoned, his pants redone. Except for the lack of tie, he looked exactly as he had done when he'd first walked into the restaurant. As though nothing had happened. As though past minutes hadn't existed.

They might have just shared cake and coffee, instead of their bodies.

"I have a meeting to get to," he said, his voice as unaffected as his exterior. "You may stay here if you wish. The room is paid for through the night."

"I…I…"

"That is all I will be requiring from you. Though, I confess, I didn't expect you to give in quite so easily."

His words were cold, distant, and she tried to recapture the feeling she'd had moments ago, of feeling close to him, and found she couldn't. She would wonder if it had all been in her mind except she was still naked, on the bed.

She sat up, holding her hands over as much of her body as she could. Trying to reclaim some modesty, some dignity, some…something.

"I would have taken a lot less from you, *cara mia*, but you played the part of whore so well, who was I to stop you?"

She felt as if she'd been slapped, a sick, cold feeling of shame trickling through her veins. And she had no mask to recall. None to put in place and hide her nakedness, her vulnerability. "But you…I…"

"Speechless?" He arched a dark brow. "It was quite good, I'll give you that. But, regrettably, I don't have time for seconds." He bent and picked up his tie, tying it quickly before buttoning his jacket.

He was untouched. Invulnerable. And she was still stripped. Of everything.

"As I said, I require nothing more from you. Consider your debt paid." He turned away from her. "The sex was… incredible. But I'm not sure it was worth a million dollars.

I think, in the end, you got the better part of the deal." He strode away from her, pulling the door open and pausing, turning to face her. "I want you to remember something, Charity."

He waited. Waited until her heart was thundering so hard she was certain he could hear it. Waited until she was certain she would be ill. Waited until she couldn't hold the question back any longer.

"What?" she asked, her throat dry.

"That it was just as I said. I made you beg for it." Then he walked through the door, and let it close firmly behind him.

Charity just sat there in the center of the bed, tugging her legs up to her chest. She looked down at the white bedspread and saw a smear of blood and the full horror hit her.

A tear slid down her cheek, a sob shaking her body.

Dear God, what had she done? What had he made her into?

She'd never been a "good girl." Never been honorable or honest. How could you be when the first skill you learned was tricking strangers into thinking you needed money so you could bring it back to your father? How could you ever be good when you'd been straddling the lines between right and wrong from the beginning?

But there were lines she had never crossed. She had never used her body like this.

And now...

The room is paid for...

No. She wouldn't stay here. She couldn't. And she wouldn't let that damned lingerie touch her skin ever again.

Another tear slipped down her cheek and she wiped it away, anger fueling her now. She could fall apart later, but for now, she needed to handle this.

She had made a mistake. A terrible mistake. She had

revealed herself to him. Her real self, not just her facade. You didn't show yourself to a mark, ever.

He was still a mark. That was all. And she would never make such a mistake again.

She picked up the phone that was by the bedside and dialed the front desk. "Yes," she said when the woman on the other end answered. "I'm in Mr. Amari's room. I need a pair of sweats and a T-shirt. Medium. Some sneakers. Size eight. And a bra. Thirty-six B. Just charge it to the room."

She hung up and sat back down on the bed. She wasn't touching that dress, those shoes, or the lingerie again.

The sweats were a fair trade.

It was the last thing she would ever take from Rocco Amari. The very last thing.

After this, she would forget about him. About this hotel room. Where she had lost her pride and her virginity all at the same time.

From this moment on, Rocco Amari was dead to her. She would leave this experience here, over and done.

She'd used her body to escape, so she would damn well see that it was an escape. No more cons. No more helping her father out with one last thing.

She would leave here, and go into her new life, with a fresh start.

After this, she would not speak of him. She would not think of him. She would take nothing from him ever again.

CHAPTER THREE

ROCCO AMARI WAS a bastard. In every sense of the word. He'd been aware of that from an early age. From the time he'd first been teased by other neighborhood children for not having a father to the moment he'd watched his mother, a grim look of wounded pride on her face, accept money from an employee of the man who'd sired him, to help them keep the modest house they called home. Provided they never made contact with him.

Yes, he had known, then and always, that he was nothing more than an illegitimate child born to a rich man's unwanted mistress. And as time had gone on he had learned that playing the part of the bastard in the colloquial sense served a man well in his ascent to success.

Though, in his case, the role had become his reality. There was no place in his life for conscience, no place for compassion. He had learned, long ago, that a man had to look out for himself because when push came to shove no one else would.

Venture capital was not the sort of business that lent itself to being sentimental or soft. Yes, it was about building businesses, but you had to be willing to cut dead branches. And Rocco was more than willing.

A man had to protect what was his, because other men wouldn't hesitate to try and claim it for themselves.

And given that he was a bastard, and given that he took a dim view of compassion, he found himself irritated by the fact that the conscience he had no place for felt seared by his encounter with Charity Wyatt.

He had never meant for it to go so far.

The plan had been to bring her into the hotel room, strip her bare, humiliate her and leave. Perhaps, not an overly sympathetic plan, but nowhere in his planning had he imagined he would actually... No. Trading sex for his stolen money had never been a part of the plan. Yes, he had intended to flirt with the line. He had always intended to do that. But Charity was a thief, and in his mind she was just lucky he didn't believe in more medieval forms of punishment.

But things had not gone according to his plan. He had lost control.

Which was, perhaps, the most unforgivable part about it.

The rest he could have forgiven himself for. But not the loss of control.

By taking her to his room, by commanding her to strip, by making her beg for him, he had been proving to her that she was in over her head. That he commanded the situation, as he did all things. But her rich, dark eyes had met him in challenge as she'd taken the expensive, overtly sexual clothing off her body, revealing the perfection beneath. And something had flipped. He had not proven his control. She had *broken* it. Yes, he was certain he had humiliated her, but at what cost? At what cost to his own pride?

It had been nearly two months since their encounter, yet at night he still woke up drenched in a cold sweat, dreaming of soft delicate fingertips trailing down his stomach. Of rich, dark curls spread out over his chest. Coal-black eyes looking up at him with wonder.

It was the wonder that got him. Because it wasn't anything he had never seen before. Certainly, women had looked at him with desire, with satisfaction, but never with the kind of awe he had seen in Charity's eyes. And he knew why.

He clenched his hand into a fist. He shouldn't care. What did it matter if a woman had made love to a hundred men, or one? It didn't. It shouldn't. Not to a man like him.

And yet it mattered.

It made his sin feel that much greater, when he didn't wish to feel as though he had sinned at all. Normally, he lived his life exactly the way he chose to, conducting affairs with women as he saw fit, spending his money as he chose, drinking as much as he desired. He didn't answer to anyone, least of all the archaic idea of black-and-white morality. Life on the streets of Rome had taught him early on that morality was only for the middle class.

Those who had nothing couldn't afford it, and those with billions could pay to bypass it.

And yet here he was, regretting a sexual encounter with all the guilt of a choir boy. Concerning himself over the virginity of a woman who had been far from *innocent* regardless of her past sexual experience.

It was unacceptable as far as he was concerned. As it was unacceptable that the woman was still taking up so much space in his mind. It was also unacceptable that he was still without his money.

He had not intended to let her off the hook on that score, either.

But as he had deviated from his plan, he had yet to regroup and decide what he would do now.

He could not pursue prosecution now. As he had promised absolution in exchange for sex. However, he'd never intended to actually have sex with her.

But he had. And that limited his options.

That damned conscience again. Where the hell had it come from? He should have no qualms about either one of those things.

His intercom buzzed and he pressed it, annoyance coursing through his veins. "What?"

"Mr. Amari—" his secretary, Nora, sounded harried "—there is a woman here who refuses to leave."

Rocco gritted his teeth. This was not the first time, nor, he imagined, would it be the last. It was either Elizabeth, a woman he'd ended his association with a little over three months ago, or it was someone entirely random, hoping to fill the currently vacant position of mistress in his life.

Too bad for whoever it was he didn't enjoy being pursued. He liked to be the one directing the pursuit.

"Tell her I am in no mood."

"I did. She is still sitting here."

"Then have security remove her."

"I thought I should call you before I resorted to that," Nora said, her tone conveying that she found the idea of having a woman forcibly removed from the building distasteful. He didn't find it distasteful in the least. If she didn't want to be carted out, then she should have obeyed the command to leave in the first place.

"Next time don't bother. Have security remove her as a matter of course. You have my permission."

He heard a muffled shout, and response from Nora. She must have put her hand over the receiver. And then she was back. "Mr. Amari, she says her name is Charity Wyatt, and she says you will want to see her."

His blood ran cold. Rage following closely, thawing out the ice.

He didn't want to see Charity Wyatt unless it was in hell.

Of course, in many ways he felt he was already there.

Put there by his very own fallen angel. Who had now crawled back into the pit to pay him a visit.

"Send her up," he said, shutting off the intercom. He would regret this. And yet, he couldn't resist the temptation. To see her one more time. To shove her skirt up around her hips and take her again, bent over his desk this time. To prove that she was just as helpless in the face of this attraction as he was. Prove that he wasn't weak.

He stood from behind his desk and began to pace the room, pausing as soon as he heard a knock on the door. A timid knock. Clearly, Charity Wyatt was not quite so defiant as she had been the last time they met.

She wasn't defiant for long. She melted quickly enough beneath your touch.

He gritted his teeth and willed his body back into submission. "Come in."

The door opened, and the sight that greeted him was a surprise. It was Charity, but not as he had ever seen her before. Gone was the beautiful, sleek siren he had taken to bed in the hotel suite. Instead, standing in front of him was a woman wearing black pants and a T-shirt. Her dark wavy hair was pulled back into a ponytail that looked as if it would suit a schoolgirl better than a woman in her early twenties.

The only makeup she appeared to be wearing was a smear of gloss over her lips, the rest of her face bare. There were dark circles under her eyes, as though she hadn't slept.

One thing was certain; she was not here to conduct a seduction.

He fought against the hard punch of disappointment that slammed into his gut. He shouldn't care. He would listen to whatever it was she had to say, and go out and find the nearest socialite and drag her back to his penthouse.

That was his problem. He had been working himself into the ground since his encounter with Charity, and he had not had a chance to be with anyone in the time since. Nearly two months was far too long for a man like him.

Still standing there looking wide-eyed and wounded, she made his gut twist hard. She was not supposed to be here, this woman who had destroyed his control.

He needed her gone.

"Well, obviously you aren't here to screw me. Which makes me feel very short on patience," he said. "You had better speak quickly."

She met his gaze, completely unintimidated by his attempt at scaring her away. "I am certainly not here to… That," she said, her tone haughty.

He let out a heavy sigh, looking down at the paperweight on his desk. Straightening it before looking at her again. "I find myself growing more impatient. Either get on your knees for me or get out."

"There are no circumstances on earth that would find me on my knees for you. Not begging you, not pleasuring you. That is my firm promise."

Anger cut through his veins like a knife. "We will see about that; or do you forget that I hold your future in my hands?"

She crossed her arms beneath her breasts and tilted her head to the side, that ridiculous ponytail tilting with her, glossy dark curls sweeping over her shoulders. "Before you start making threats you should know that I carry *your* future in my womb."

Charity hadn't meant to impart the news quite that way.

She had intended to come over slightly more vulnerable. That was the entire point behind coming in her waitressing outfit. The entire point to not dressing up, to show him the way that she really lived.

Maybe it was stupid to try and engender his sympathy, for a second time, but she needed him to understand that she wasn't living large with his money. Because his money was exactly what she needed.

For her new life. For her.

For the baby.

It was still so surreal. More surreal than sleeping with a stranger at all, was the realization that she had created a life with one. That there would be a person on earth who would share DNA that belonged in part to her, and in part to him. It didn't seem fair, really. Not to her, not to the child. She didn't much care if it was fair to Rocco.

There were certain things she could never provide for a child, not with her income. And really, she shouldn't be ashamed. This was a sacrifice of her pride, to ensure that her child was taken care of. To ensure the child had everything it deserved.

She didn't want him to play the part of daddy, and try to make a happy family with her. Far from it. She just needed his money.

But, she felt she had a legitimate claim on it, considering.

She ignored the slight jab in her conscience that reminded her she had already taken some of his money.

But I don't have it. And so neither will the baby.

She needed the baby to have it. Otherwise, what could she offer? It was either life with the server's wages, or life that looked a lot like hers had when she'd been growing up. Moving from place to place, running cons.

She didn't want that for her child. She wanted better. She wanted the best. She wanted to try and figure out how to be a good mother. She wanted to figure out how to be something other than a thief.

It had been nearly thirty seconds since she had dropped her bombshell, and Rocco still hadn't spoken. Charity didn't feel obligated to fill the silence. He deserved to feel the same shock she had felt when she had taken the test. When she had seen the little pink lines that had changed everything.

Yes, they had used a condom, but she knew enough to know that they did fail sometimes. And anyway, no amount of arguing that point with the universe would take back what had been done.

Still, she couldn't help but feel she was being punished for the way she'd handled things. Had she refused him, she would simply be in jail rather than expecting a baby.

That thought almost made her laugh. Just because it was so absurd. Just because she could hardly feel any regrets over sidestepping prison. No matter what else had happened since.

In some ways, she had arrived in a hopeful place about the baby. That this would be a true stepping-stone into something different. Into a different life.

"Was that your way of making an announcement?" Rocco finally spoke, his tone hard.

"I suppose it was. That wasn't exactly the plan, but then I didn't expect you to be so horrible. I suppose that was my first mistake. We have met after all."

"We used protection," he said, the words cold. Blunt.

"Yes, and I did speak to the universe about that when I realized my period was late. However, it didn't seem to care."

"How do I know you didn't rush out and bed the first man you found after we parted? A little bit of revenge? Trying to pass his baby off as mine?"

Charity embraced the genuine, righteous anger that burned through her. "How dare you? You, who blackmailed me into sex. You took my virginity in payment for money my *father* stole, money that I never touched." That much was true. She'd never had her hands on the money for a moment. "You are every inch the villain in this scenario, Rocco Amari. I will not lie down and take these accusations. I will not allow you to stand there looking superior when the simple fact is you all but forced me into having sex with you, and you don't deserve to comment on my character when you were the one who led things between us."

Rocco drew back as though he had been slapped. But when he recovered, she could feel the rage radiating from him in waves. "Perhaps I did some of those things. But I did not force you into bed. Do not deny that in the end you *begged* for me. You said yes. Yes *please*. And I gave you what you wanted."

She looked away, her cheeks heating. "I was a virgin. It was never going to take much to make me lose my head. I wouldn't let it go to your ego." She needed him to feel responsible. And she needed him to feel annoyed. So he would get rid of her, but also offer her money.

"You cannot play the victim now. I would never have gone so far with you had you not asked."

"Are you honestly going to say that you didn't intend for it to end in sex?"

He paused, his dark eyes flat, his jaw clenched tight. "I did not. All I really wanted was for you to beg. But you were much more convincing than I anticipated."

The admission seemed to cost him, and she had no idea why. If it should hurt anyone to hear that, it was her.

She had overpaid. And now, she would keep on paying.

She gritted her teeth. "Don't forget you begged, too."

"I didn't have to beg for long, did I?"

"I *hate you*," she said, and she found she meant every word, even though she was speaking it as part of her role. As part of the indignant, downtrodden waitress who found herself alone and pregnant.

That's exactly what you are.

She swallowed hard, her throat tightening, genuine emotion overwhelming her. "What have you done to us?" she asked.

"Inexperience will not cover your actions in this. Do not put the blame on me entirely."

"Oh, you don't want all the blame? Then perhaps you shouldn't swan around as though you are the God of the universe. You cannot be both all-powerful and without fault. You threatened me, you made me feel as though I had to fall into line or I would be put in jail. Yes, I acknowledge that in the end I consented. But had I not been coerced in the first place I would never have been in your room. Obviously, I have spent my life staying away from men's hotel rooms, and yours would have been no exception."

"Fine. I was an absolute monster. Is that what you want to hear? Does that ease your pain? It shouldn't, as it doesn't change the situation."

"I'm surprised you would admit to the fact that you're a monster," she said, anger pouring through her.

"Being considered a nice man has never been a concern of mine. I don't particularly care whether or not I acted with the highest moral standards. That is not what drives me. I wanted success. I have achieved it. And I will keep it. Everything else is incidental. I will have what's mine, and that is my utmost concern."

"I can't get you your money back. I don't know where my father is. If I did, count on it, I would be the first person to turn him in. I'm not protecting him. I'm not that self-sacrificial. In fact, I'm not self-sacrificial at all. I slept with you to keep myself out of trouble because you wouldn't listen to me. I would have turned him in to you a thousand times over to avoid that." The only problem with turning her father in was that he would talk. And then her proclamations of innocence wouldn't mean much anymore. Because he would confirm her involvement and she didn't want that. Even though Rocco didn't believe her innocence she couldn't bring herself to confess her guilt, either.

"All of this is beside the point," he said, waving his hand, as though to brush her concerns out of the air as if they were nothing more important or substantial than cobwebs. "What do you want?"

"I wanted to give you the chance to know about the baby. Because I wanted to give you the chance to make a choice about whether or not you wanted to be in its life."

He only stared at her, dark eyes flat. "And what part would you expect me to play in the life of a child?"

"The part of father I would imagine, as that is the role you played in its conception." He wouldn't accept it. And she knew it. But she had to ask. She'd never known her mother, and her father had been distant. She would give Rocco this chance.

But he would turn it down. And she would be grateful. Because while she needed to give him a chance to be involved with his child, the last thing she wanted was for him to have any involvement with her.

Beyond the financial support he would no doubt offer, and which she and her baby would desperately need.

"I would not know the first thing about being a father. I didn't have one."

"Well, I don't have a mother, and yet it seems I'm about to become one. Apparently, lacking a particular parent isn't an effective form of birth control. Who knew?"

"I do not see why you would want me to participate in the child's life."

She was surprised by the depth of anger she felt when he said those words. Surprised by the deep, elemental rage that started down low in her stomach and flowed outward. Because she was only just wrapping her head around this motherhood thing, and that she should have an instinct, of any kind, was shocking. Especially because her ultimate goal was definitely not to have him involved.

But hearing him say it—it affected something in her she hadn't even known was there. It cut too close to the bone. Too close to her own childhood. So full of indifference, abandonment, regret…

She gritted her teeth. "Then don't. But you will pay child support. I'm not raising your child in poverty while you eat in fine dining establishments and…and…prop your feet up in your giant Italian villa."

"I most certainly will pay child support. If it is mine."

"It *is* yours. I haven't been with another man. Ever. My first time was in your godforsaken hotel suite, and it was my only time." She swallowed hard. "And you know that. I *know* you do. You, on the other hand, have been with so many women I bet you don't even know the official number. I made sure to get a panel done when I went in for my blood test to confirm the pregnancy. To make sure that I didn't catch anything from you."

His lip curled into a sneer. "I always use protection."

"And obviously it isn't always effective."

His expression went flat again. Unaffected. "Do you need money for medical care?"

She blinked. "I will. Unless I can get on some kind of assistance…"

"How soon can you get a paternity test done?"

She clenched her hands into fists, starting to feel light-headed. "Not for a few weeks. And from what I've heard there's a miscarriage risk."

"Your choice. Discuss it with your physician at your appointment, and I will leave that decision to you. But, if you do take assistance from me during the pregnancy and upon delivery of the child the test is done and I discover it is not mine, you will owe me for the care you received."

She gritted her teeth. "I will probably take option two, as I'm completely confident in what the results will be. I'm not worried about owing you a damn thing."

"Excellent," he said, as though they had just solved a particularly tricky business issue. "I will arrange for an account to be set up for your medical needs. After the delivery of the baby, after we have legally established paternity, we can work out some sort of child support agreement."

This was it. She had won. He was agreeing to child support. It was going to get her what she needed, give her and her child the best life possible. And he wasn't going to be involved.

For some reason, the victory was so much more hollow than she had imagined it might be. For some reason, she didn't feel victorious at all. She just felt dizzy, dazed.

Maybe because she was in shock. She very likely had been from the moment she'd first taken the pregnancy tests. The first one, at home, and the follow-up blood work at the free clinic. She had probably been in shock the whole time she was formulating this plan. A way to make sure everything was taken care of, without having Rocco in her life.

It was difficult to feel victorious when everything about this just felt frightening. Strange.

"I suppose you know how to contact me," she said.

"And you know how to contact me. Clearly."

"Is that everything?"

He shrugged and went to sit behind his desk. "Unless you have any further concerns. Or, have any information on the whereabouts of your father."

She shook her head, feeling numb. "No."

"That is a shame. Do let me know when the results of the paternity test are in."

"You mean when your child is born."

"I imagine the timing will coincide," he said, looking away from her now completely. As though she was already gone.

"I'll call you. Someone. Your secretary," she said, turning away from him and walking out the door.

She managed to hold it together until she was halfway through the lobby. But then, just as she was passing the receptionist's desk, a sob worked its way through her frame, catching her breath, making her pause. Her chest burned, her whole body shaking. She didn't know why this hurt so much. Didn't know why it mattered whether or not he cared about the child. She didn't want him to, dammit. Why was she feeling guilty now?

Because you know how much it hurts. You know it hurts forever.

Yes, she did know. Knew that the pain of abandonment, of complete disinterest, didn't ease.

She hated that her child would be starting out life the way she had started hers. And it was a strange and terrifying thing to know that, already, the needs of her child felt so much more important than her own.

She pressed on through the lobby, sucking in a gasp of fresh air as soon as she was outside. She blinked against the harsh light of the sun, staring up at the cloudless blue sky that seemed to mock the state of her life with its beautiful perfection.

But somehow, while part of her felt angry about the

beauty of the day, another part of her took comfort in it. Things were changing in her life, faster than she could process them. But everything around her was the same.

It wasn't the end of the world. It was just the start of a strange, new one. And no, her child wouldn't have a father. But she knew from experience that a father who sucked was probably worse than no father at all.

And her child would have a mother. There was no question about that.

It was scary. Terrifying. She was a twenty-two-year-old waitress who didn't feel as if she'd started her life yet. She didn't know how to be normal. Her moral compass skewed from childhood. But she would have to change the way she saw things now, change the way she did things. Because she didn't want to carry on the legacy that her father had tried to instill in her. A legacy she had been taking part in because she hadn't known what else to do.

She still didn't know what to do. But with the financial support coming from Rocco, she wouldn't even be tempted to engage in cons anymore. Maybe she would get a house in the country. Maybe she would make friends with other mothers. Maybe she would make up a story about where she was from, and what happened to her baby's father.

Maybe that could be her last con. One that she lived in. One that she stayed in. Something normal, something happy.

The thought of it made her smile.

Things were going to change. But she needed that. Desperately. *She* needed to change. Maybe this was her chance to finally have real connections. To love someone the way she wanted to. Without reserve. With love in return.

A love neither she nor her child would ever have to earn.

No *just one more con* looming overhead. A mythical

destination that would supposedly fix all, but would never arrive.

She closed her eyes and wiped away the tears that had fallen down her cheeks. She didn't need Rocco Amari to be happy. Neither did her child.

This whole thing with her dad had started out as one of the biggest mistakes of her life. But maybe out of it something amazing would happen.

Either way, it was a new chapter. She was done with her father. She was done with the life they'd led. Done with cheating people.

And she was done with Rocco, except when it came to the financial support he would offer. It was a new life, a new beginning.

And now that she had taken care of the hard part, she was ready to start.

CHAPTER FOUR

THE ROOM WAS EMPTY. Everything was gone. Nothing to identify who might live in this tiny little house in Rome. No toys to show that a child played here. No pots or pans in the kitchen to prove that there was a mother who lived here. A mother who had cooked dinner every night, regardless if the meal was comprised of the most modest portions.

Even the blankets that were usually fashioned into a nest in the corner of the living area were gone.

And there were strangers standing there. Strangers who were smiling although there was nothing to smile about.

His toys were gone.

But worst of all, his mother was gone.

No matter how many times he asked where she was, no one would answer. He asked until he was hoarse, until his voice was gone, and still there was no answer. Only smiling, and strange assurances that everything would be fine, when he knew nothing would ever be fine again.

The room was empty, and he couldn't find anything that he needed.

Rocco woke up, his body drenched in sweat, his heart hammering so hard he feared it might burst through his chest. His bedroom was, of course, not empty. He was sleeping on a king-size bed with lush blankets and pillows covering every square inch. In the corner, he could see his dresser, and mounted to the wall the flat-screen TV. Everything was here, just as it should be.

Most importantly, he was not a small crying child. He was a man. And he was not helpless.

Yet for some reason, in spite of the realization that he had been having his usual dream, the unease didn't let up. His chest still felt as though it was being squeezed tight, a large hand wrapped around his throat.

He got out of bed and walked over to the bar that was next the door. He needed a drink, and then he could go back to sleep.

He flipped on the light and reached for a bottle of Scotch, pouring himself a generous amount, his hands shaking. As he lifted the glass to his lips, he replayed the dream in his mind. And suddenly the face of the child changed. It wasn't him any longer, but a child with her mother's defiant expression and wavy black hair.

He swore and slammed the glass down onto the bar top. There was no reason for him to take part in the life of the child Charity was carrying. The odds that she was truly pregnant were slim. The odds that she was carrying his child slimmer still. It was a tactic to use him. She was a con woman, just like her father, and he knew it.

Yes, she had been a virgin, he knew that, too. But perhaps she had not been. Perhaps it was all part of her elaborate ruse. He couldn't be sure.

He should forget this. Forget she had ever come to see him. It would be easy for him to send a certain amount of money to her every month, money he would never even look at. She would be cared for, as would the baby, and he could go on as he always had.

Yet again, his mind was filled with large, sad brown eyes. He looked down into the Scotch as though it betrayed him, then lifted the glass and hurled it at the wall, watching it shatter. It left a dark blot behind, a spray of liquid clearly visible, and shards of glass on the floor. He didn't care.

And he shouldn't care about Charity Wyatt and the baby she might or might not be carrying.

You would abandon your child? Is this what you have become?

He did not hear the questions in his own voice, but a voice from far in the past. His mother. Who had left luxury with his father to give birth to him. Who had, before that, sold all of her jewelry, all of her clothes. A mother who had worked nights at a factory, walking a dangerous route home in the early hours, alone.

His mother had given her all, until she had lost her life in pursuit of caring for him.

And he was going to leave his child with nothing more than an automatic deposit once a month.

He ignored the uncharacteristic guilt that wound itself around his lungs, making it difficult to breathe. He didn't believe in guilt. It was useless. It accomplished nothing. He believed in action.

So take action.

What action could he take? Would he keep the child for himself? Take Charity as his wife? Make a family with the woman who had defrauded him out of a million dollars?

The woman who had tested his control and found it wanting?

Unacceptable.

All of it. He owed her nothing. He didn't even owe her child support all things considered. He was still half convinced she had his money tucked away somewhere. A million dollars of his ferreted away into an account to use at her discretion.

In truth, he was being generous offering her anything. Yes, he was generous.

He took another glass from the bar and poured himself more Scotch. He would not think of this again. He would place his assistant in charge of arranging Charity's medical appointments. She would receive the best care available. Another token of his generosity.

He had made the right decision. And he would not question it again.

He downed to the rest of his Scotch and went back to bed.

Charity felt like hell. She had for the past two weeks. Everything she ate seemed to disagree with her, and she had no energy at all. She had missed so many shifts at the restaurant that her financial situation was getting dire.

But, the unavoidable fact was that nobody wanted a clammy, pale waitress serving them food.

And today was her first official doctor's appointment that had been arranged at the clinic chosen by Rocco. It was a strange thing, going to a clinic that had been selected by the man who was so intent on keeping himself separate from all of this.

Well, she was willing to bet that Rocco himself hadn't actually selected the clinic. More likely he had had his assistant do it. Which, actually sat a bit easier with her.

The place was certainly upscale, a far cry from the free clinic where she'd gone to get her blood work done in the early stages of the pregnancy. Instead of plastic chairs, cracked tile floors and water-stained ceilings there was plush carpet, a comfortable seating area designed to look more like the living room of a nice home and chilled bottles of water offered upon entry.

It was amazing what could be achieved with a little bit

of money. Or a lot of money, in this case. She could almost see why her father was so driven to join the elite class and enjoy the fruits of their labor.

Of course, Charity had discovered that it wasn't really worth the risk. Too little too late, however.

"Ms. Wyatt?" A woman poked her head through one of the doors that partitioned the waiting area off from the patient rooms.

Charity picked up her water bottle and stood, following the woman back to a scale, where her weight was taken, then to a restroom, where a sample was taken. And from there, to one of the little rooms that had a white gown neatly folded on a chair and a large cushioned exam table at the center.

"The doctor will be in to see you shortly. Remove your clothes, and put the gown on," the woman said.

Charity nodded, feeling slightly numb again. The baby stuff was all fine in theory, but when things got real like this she started to retreat inside herself again.

She went through the motions, removing her clothing, putting the thin nondescript gown on. She sat on the table, her hands folded in her lap, unease pooling in her stomach.

There was a knock on the door. "Come in," she said.

A smiling woman in a lab coat walked through the door, and Charity smiled back. And then a man followed her, dressed in a perfectly fitted black suit, his black hair combed off his forehead, his dark eyes glittering with some sort of intense emotion she could not readily identify. One she didn't want to identify. Any more than she wanted to identify the man himself.

Rocco was here. And she felt as though she had been punched.

"Well, now that the father is here, I suppose we're ready to begin," the doctor said.

"Such a surprise," Charity said, her hackles rising. "Rocco," she said, his first name strange on her lips, "I didn't expect you."

"I would imagine not. *I* didn't expect me. And yet, here I am." He didn't sound very happy about it.

She smoothed the gown down, ensuring that it covered as much of her legs as possible. "I don't really see how it's possible for you to surprise yourself."

She was shocked, but she was doing her best not to let him see it. She promised herself she wouldn't give him any more of who she was. He didn't deserve it. A mark never did. And he had already had enough of her.

"We live in strange and interesting times," he said, taking a seat in one of the chairs that sat opposite the exam table.

The doctor looked from her to Rocco, and back to her.

"Everything is fine," Rocco said, not bothering to look at Charity. "Just a little spat."

Charity snorted. "Yes, a lover's quarrel." What a joke. She and Rocco could hardly be called lovers. They'd had sex. At its most base level. Love hadn't come into it. Like hadn't even been involved. He had used her. Humiliated her.

"So what is it that we are waiting for?" Rocco said, looking around as though he was expecting something grand, as though she was going to deliver the baby here and now.

The doctor blinked, then turned to the computer, entering a password, and bringing up Charity's chart. "Well, Charity, your weight looks good. And everything was normal with the urine sample."

Ridiculous, considering Rocco had seen her naked, but the mention of *fluids* made Charity's cheeks heat. "Well, that's good to know."

"And, now we're just going to try and see if we can hear a heartbeat. If we can't get it on the Doppler, it could just be because it's so early. So there's no need to be concerned. But it is nice to try and establish viability this way if we can."

Rocco was staring at her, hard. Maybe this was what he was here for. The chance to hear the heartbeat. To see if she was telling the truth. Though, she would have thought that he might send a lackey to ascertain this sort of information. She could just picture his secretary sitting here, waiting to report back. She would find that less disconcerting.

The doctor stood and put on a pair of rubber gloves. "Could you lie down please?"

Charity shot a look over to Rocco. "Please come and stand up by my shoulders."

"You did not conceive the baby on your own," he said, his tone laconic. "We both know I've seen it before."

Even the doctor blinked at him in shock. "You will have to forgive him," Charity said. "He was raised by wolves. They did a terrible job."

Rocco shrugged, a rather wolfish smile crossing his features. "The founder of Rome was also raised by wolves. I consider myself in good company."

Charity rolled her eyes. "Oh, great Caesar, come and stand up by my shoulders."

She was surprised when he complied. But maybe he was just tired of the delay. He moved up to the head of the exam table, and she lay down. The doctor retrieved a sheet from beneath the cabinet and laid it over Charity's lap.

The doctor adjusted the gown, then squirted some warm gel onto Charity's stomach. She took a small wand and placed it over the gel, sliding it around, a strange, watery sound filling the room. She moved it lower, and lower still. And suddenly a pulsing sound rose up over the baseline noise.

"That's it," the doctor said, her tone bright. "That's the baby's heartbeat."

Charity looked up at Rocco, then immediately wished she hadn't. She didn't care what his reaction was. At least, she shouldn't care. But truly, she had imagined he would have no reaction at all, and that was clearly not the case.

His face had turned to stone, as hard and immobile as a statue.

He was truly beautiful, and it was an inconvenient moment to think of it. But he was the father of her baby and that realization made her study his features that much more closely. The golden tone to his skin, the hard, angular lines of his cheekbones, his jaw. The sensual curve of his mouth.

Her child would be half of him. Would he have the same sulky expression? Dark straight hair like his father? Or a riot of black curls like her?

Rocco's frown deepened. "It does not sound like a heartbeat," he said, the mocking edge smoothed from his voice. He sounded...strange. Uncertain.

"It does to me," the doctor said, clearly not at all intimidated by Rocco.

There was an odd light in Rocco's dark eyes, something she couldn't put a name to. "It's very fast," he said, and if Charity wasn't so cynical about him, she might have thought she heard concern in his voice.

"Normal," the doctor said. "Strong, and absolutely nothing to worry about." She directed her focus to Charity.

"She is pregnant," Rocco said, not a question.

The doctor's brows shot up again. "Absolutely."

A deep groove formed between his dark brows. "I see," he said, his tone stoic now. "And I hear."

For a while, no one spoke at all. There was only the

sound of the baby's heartbeat, and on the monitor, a wavy line that moved with each beat. A band that seemed to stretch between Rocco and herself, tightening a bond between them she hadn't realized was there.

Charity wished it would go away.

"Do you have any questions for me?" the doctor asked, breaking into Charity's internal monologue.

Charity shook her head, suddenly unable to say anything. Unable to think at all.

"Then I'll see you in four weeks for your next appointment. Everything seems right on schedule. Nothing to worry about." Charity could think of about fifty things to worry about without even trying.

The doctor removed the wand from her stomach and wiped away the gel with the sheet that was over her lap. "I'll leave you to get dressed."

And then she left, leaving Charity and Rocco alone.

"Would you go please?"

"Why?" Rocco asked, sitting back down in the chair he had been in before. Any softening, any humanity she thought she might have glimpsed a moment ago was gone now.

"I need to get dressed."

He put his hands behind his head and leaned back. "You're being so charmingly modest. We both know you possess quite a bit more boldness."

"Fine. If you're looking for a show, enjoy." She stood from the exam table, letting the sheet fall to the floor. The gown covered her until she turned her back on him, and she knew she was revealing everything to him then. She untied the top of the gown and let it fall completely. Then she set about getting dressed.

She was too angry to be embarrassed. She didn't care

if he looked. He was right, he had already seen her. He had touched her. He was the reason things were like this.

Once all of her clothing was on, she turned to face him. He was staring at her, dark eyes glittering. "I should've charged admission for that," she said.

"I found the ingénue much more charming. Perhaps you could revert back?"

"Oh, I think you and I both know that I can't play the ingénue now. I seem to have lost my innocence somewhere."

A half smile curved his lips. "And so you have. Though, I'm starting to think that virginity is not necessarily innocence."

She shrugged. "I won't argue with you there."

"Is this an admission of guilt?"

"Certainly not. I'm only saying my innocence is unconnected to whether or not I've slept with a man."

"You really were a virgin, weren't you?"

She lifted her chin, staring him down. "Is it important?"

He looked back at her, and for a moment she thought she saw something in his dark gaze, something that looked strikingly like guilt. But then it was gone, replaced with the smooth, impenetrable expression she'd come to expect from him. "Not particularly. If I had a conscience, I suppose it might be a little dented by the realization. Happy for both of us I don't. Though, it might bear weight on how convinced I am that this is my child," he said, directing his gaze at her stomach.

"It is your child. There was no one else before you, and no one else after you." She watched his expression carefully for more clues. And was disappointed. So she pushed harder. "Makes it difficult for you to vilify me, doesn't it?"

"You might find this strange," he said, his tone hard. "But I'm not here to vilify you."

"Well, you certainly aren't here to shower me with flowers and compliments. So why are you here?"

"I've changed my mind."

"What do you mean you've changed your mind?"

He stood, pacing the room. "I have decided the child support isn't enough. I have decided that I want my child." He paused, dark eyes boring into hers. "Not only do I want my child, I want you."

CHAPTER FIVE

HE HAD SUCCEEDED in shocking her. She was simply staring at him, her large, dark eyes wide, her lush lips parted.

"Was there something confusing about what I just said?" he asked.

He felt a twinge of something in his stomach. A slight bit of… Had he been any other man he might have thought it was insecurity. But that was impossible. Still, he was questioning his methods. He did not seem to be winning her over to his side with his current tactic.

But he despised the need to try and woo her. Especially considering that he still believed her to be a thief. But, perhaps treating her so harshly was not helpful.

He decided to try something slightly different. "What I mean to say is, I am keeping the child. And I am keeping you as well, as I find the idea of our child being without a mother unacceptable. I am still missing a million dollars. I do not feel as though keeping you in exchange is unreasonable."

Her expression contorted, this time anger replacing shock.

He had the feeling he had not selected the proper method.

"You can't…keep me. What does that even mean? You cannot *keep* a person."

He frowned. "Certainly I can. I have a villa on the Amalfi Coast. And I intend to take you there."

"You cannot be serious."

"I am serious. I'm very serious. In fact, I intend to take you at once."

"I can't leave," she said, her dark eyes shifting to the left. "Who will feed my cat?"

"You have a cat?"

She met his gaze again, her expression ferocious. "No, but I could."

"There, you have no cat. There is no issue. It's settled. You are leaving with me. Now."

She blinked rapidly. "What about my job?"

"What about your job?" he said, waving his hand. "You are a waitress. And as the mother of my child, you will never have to wait tables again."

"I don't understand. Just a couple of weeks ago you sent me away, promising me no contact, and money." She sounded desperate and angry.

Yes, he had said all that. But at the time he'd been knocked so flat by her revelation his reaction had been... much less than gracious. And he'd decided he didn't believe her, because it was easier. She couldn't be pregnant, not by him. Not when he'd used a condom.

He had decided that she probably wasn't pregnant at all. But then the dreams of that wide-eyed little girl had continued to plague him. And so he'd decided to come down to the doctor's appointment and prove it.

But Charity had been at the appointment. And then... and then the heartbeat.

And he had known in that moment it was his child. Had believed that, in this instance, she spoke the truth.

But he didn't want her to be too confident in that just yet. Not while he was still sorting through his feelings.

"And you seemed to want me in the child's life."

"I don't need you in the child's life," she said, "I only need child support."

"I disagree."

"You said that you didn't want to be a father," she said.

"And yet, it seems I'm going to be one. *Want* has nothing to do with it. But for stronger scruples or a stronger condom, we wouldn't be in this mess. But alas, we had neither. Still, I think the situation can be salvaged."

"I felt it had been salvaged rather well already."

"Why? Because you got my money?" Perfect, chilled rage, rushed through his veins. "What do you plan to do with the child? Farm it out to relatives? An elderly aunt? No doubt while you continued to collect my money."

"No, I intend to raise my baby. But I don't need you to do it," she said, lifting her chin, her expression defiant.

"I have as much right as you. I am the child's father."

"And, not to put too fine a point on it, I hate you."

He chuckled. "Am I supposed to be bothered by that? You are not the first woman to hate me, and I daresay you will not be the last. However, you are the first woman to carry my child. And I will have you both. This is nonnegotiable."

"Or else?" she asked, crossing her arms beneath her breasts, her dark eyes glittering.

"Prison is still an option," he ground out.

She blinked rapidly. "You wouldn't really send me to jail."

"They take very good care of pregnant women in prison." He looked at her, watched as the fear took hold of her. Good. Let her understand that he wasn't giving hollow threats. He was not a man to be trifled with. Most especially by a woman who had wronged him. "I would hate to explain to our child that its mother was a criminal, but I will do what I must."

"You bastard," she said.

"Guilty. And you might want to be careful throwing that term around, as technically, our child is a bastard, too."

Her dark eyes glittered. "How dare you?"

"That is the reality of the situation we find ourselves in, *cara mia*. If you do not like it, take steps to change it."

"What steps?"

He lifted a shoulder. "You could always marry me," he said.

It was the most extreme version of his plan, but not one he was entirely uncomfortable with. He saw no reason why marriage should affect his lifestyle in any way. Or hers. But it would at least provide a comfortable framework for his child's life. That was something he had lacked growing up, and he didn't want his child to lack in the same ways.

It was part of his growing obsession.

Ever since that night, the night after she had come to tell him about the baby, he had been plagued by the same nightmare over and over again. The empty house, the searching child. The child that eventually became his.

And he had known then what he had to do.

He had grown into an entirely selfish man over the years. He knew that. He had not connected with a single person since the death of his mother. The homes he had bounced between offered him nothing—no comfort, no love. And when he had gone into the workforce, he had approached things with a single-minded ruthlessness. Life on the street had taught him early on that you had to look out for yourself, because no one else would.

His mother's fate had taught him that you had to be the most dangerous person in the alley, or you would become a victim.

Rocco Amari refused to become a victim.

And yet, he felt connected to this child. The child in his dream. He had no way of knowing if it was a vision of some kind. In fact, he was certain it wasn't, because he didn't believe in such things. But he didn't feel he could ignore it, either.

His sleeplessness had driven him here. To confirm the pregnancy, to confirm what he must do. The moment the sound of the baby's heartbeat had filled the room, he had known. No matter the cost, he would create a family. A stable environment.

He was determined.

"Are you insane?" she asked, taking a step back.

"No."

"You say that with a lot of confidence, for someone I'm pretty certain is insane," she said, shaking her head, a curtain of glossy curls swirling around her. She truly was beautiful. It was a shame she was a criminal.

"You don't need to answer that now. But you will come back to the island with me now."

"Or prison?"

He smiled. "Or prison. Yet again, I feel it's a fairly easy choice."

"I should have run."

"Before or after the con?"

She paled, an ashen tone running beneath her cream-and-coffee skin. "I don't want to talk anymore," she said.

"Too close to the bone?"

"I don't have a choice, do I?"

He advanced on her, closing the space between them. And as the air shrank, his chest tightened, his blood running harder, faster. There was something about her, something that called to him. Something elemental. He could not fathom it.

"Did we ever?" They were not the words he meant to speak, and yet he found it was an honest question.

He wondered if there had ever been a choice where she was concerned. If, rather than being the woman he was certain had been a part of stealing his money, he had spotted her in a crowded bar, they would have ended up in bed together.

If, no matter the circumstances, their connection would have been forged.

"I didn't," she said.

"You made your choice when you agreed to help your father steal my money. And now I am the one making the choices. You will come with me. Now. I do not make empty threats, and I think you know that."

"Well then," she said, her voice strangled. "Perhaps you should show me to your private jet."

"I will. Make no mistake, *cara*, you are mine now. And by the end of next week, I will decide what exactly I am going to do with you."

For the second time Charity found herself looking at a set of written instructions, and a garment bag.

She still felt as if she was dreaming. Only, it wasn't a particularly good dream. They had left the doctor's appointment, only to get on a plane and fly overnight to Italy. Rocco had spent the entire flight ignoring her, which suited her just fine. She'd slept most of the way, and she assumed he had been working, or whatever it was he was doing on his computer. Possibly looking at pictures of women in bikinis. She didn't really care.

He'd continued his silence on the car ride through the city and up a winding mountain road. Charity had tried to appear blasé about the whole experience. From the moment they had boarded his private plane, until they had touched down in a country she had never even dreamed of visiting. But she'd found it was impossible. Especially when faced with the beauty of Italy.

The narrow streets, tall buildings, cluttered balconies and brightly colored flowers on climbing vines were too beautiful for her to ignore. She'd pressed her nose to the glass of the limo they were riding in and watched as the road widened, the buildings became more sparse, stared in awe at the intense jade ocean down at the bottom of the rocky cliffs.

And once the expansive villa had come into view, she'd had to fight to keep her mouth from dropping open.

Now she was inside, installed in her bedroom, which was larger than the New York hotel suite Rocco had seduced her in. It was expensive, light and airy, with white curtains and flowing white linens cascading over the wrought-iron frame of the bed.

And yet, there was a heaviness in her chest that she could not shake.

And now the note.

You will join me for dinner. You will wear the dress that I have provided. We have much to discuss.
—R

This scenario felt far too familiar for her liking. And the worst part was, much like the first time, she was in no position to refuse him.

She blinked, her eyes feeling gritty. The time change and restless sleep on the airplane was starting to catch up with her. She took her shirt off, and her skirt, then unzipped the garment bag to find a bright yellow dress made of a light fabric that looked as if it would be comfortable in the heat.

She had expected a corset and garter belt, so it was a pleasant surprise.

She slipped the dress on over her head and turned to look at herself in the mirror. Unfortunately, she looked as tired as she felt. Deep purple circles marked the skin beneath her eyes, and she was certain that there was a permanent line etched in her forehead that had not been there BR.

Before Rocco.

She sighed and took her hair out of its clip, running her fingers through the glossy dark curls that she had always imagined were a gift from her mother. A thick, unruly gift that made getting ready a chore. A fitting present from a woman who had never once bothered to check on the child she had given birth to.

She reached down and picked up her purse, taking out her bright pink lipstick and smearing a bit over her lips. The effect brightened her face some, made her look less tired. Made her look less worn down. She needed that. That little bit of armor in place so that he didn't just think he had won. So that he didn't assume he had the upper hand.

She arched one dark brow at her own reflection. "You are in his villa, in a foreign country. A country where you don't speak the language. He's a billionaire. And you are not even a thousandaire. There is no question who has the upper hand."

She sighed and turned away from the mirror.

She didn't know how she was going to get out of this, but she would be damned if she betrayed herself to him.

She opened the door to the bedroom, running a countdown in her mind as she walked slowly down the hallway that led to the sweeping curved staircase. She put her hand on the polished wooden banister and let her fingers glide across the smooth, cool surface as she made her way down to the opulent entryway.

Ten. Nine. Eight.

She was strong. She would hold her own.

Seven. Six. Five.

He might have brought her here, but he did not control her.

Four. Three. Two.

All of the vulnerability he had made her feel back in the hotel room was over now. She was impervious to it. Impervious to him.

One.

She stepped off the bottom stair and looked up. Rocco was there, his dark eyes clashing with hers, his hand extended toward her.

She sucked in a sharp breath, her heart hammering hard, her stomach twisting.

"So pleased you could join me," he said, appraising her slowly. "I knew that color would suit you."

"You can't imagine how relieved I am that you approve of my appearance. I was deeply concerned."

"Come now, must everything be a fight?" He kept his hand extended. "Take my hand."

"No thank you, I can walk just fine. Probably better without you leading me off a cliff. Oh, look. I suppose everything does have to be a fight."

He arched a brow and lowered his hand. "Dinner is back this way on the terrace. And while it does overlook a cliff, I have no desire to walk you off it."

"You expect me to trust you? I don't trust anyone," she said, following him through the expensive living area, her shoes loud on the marble floor.

"I see. And why is it that you don't trust anyone? Because I find that a curious stance for someone like yourself. I could understand a victim of yours no longer trusting people."

"I don't have victims," she said, her tone crisp. "They're called marks."

"Admitting something?"

"No," she said, looking away, her heart beating a bit faster, "I'm not."

"You will not convince me of your innocence. You might as well drop the denial."

She rolled her eyes. "So I should give you a full, signed confession?"

"You could start by simply answering my question."

"Why don't I trust people? Because I see what happens when you trust people. My father is a con man. He always has been. The quality time I remember with my dad consisted of running scams that required playing on people's sympathy for children. Not exactly a weekend at the ballpark. Why would I trust people?"

He pushed open the double doors that led outside to an expansive terrace that overlooked the ocean. He turned to face her, his lean figure backlit by the sun. "You shouldn't trust people. At least not in my experience. Certainly don't trust me."

She followed him outside, to a table that was set for two. There was a Mediterranean platter including olives and various other Italian delights, a basket of bread, a glass of wine for him and water for her.

"Oh, I don't trust you."

He pulled her chair out and indicated that he wanted her to sit. "Good. I don't need you to trust me. I simply need you to stay with me. Sit."

She kept her eyes on his and she obeyed his command, deciding that in this instance, it wouldn't do any good to push against him. "What do you mean you want to keep me?"

"I have done some thinking. I want to be in my child's

life. And I want you to be in the child's life. You see, I was denied both my parents at a very early age. I cannot knowingly do the same to my own flesh and blood."

"Well, I…I feel the same way. At least as far as I'm concerned." It was the truth. Growing up without a mother, it had never been an option for her to give her child up. Knowing that her mother had left her with a con artist for a father and never bothered to contact her again, had caused Charity pain all of her life. Doing the same to her own child was unthinkable.

"Then it is decided. Shall we set a wedding date?"

"I am not marrying you."

He waved a hand. "Marriage is not necessary. I'm flexible on that score. But I do think we should share a household, don't you? It would only be jarring for the child to bounce back and forth between your tiny apartment and one of my homes."

"Are you suggesting we live together?"

"If you refuse to marry me, cohabitation works just as well."

"But…I don't understand. You can't possibly want a relationship with me."

"Of course I don't." He tossed the words out casually, no venom in his tone at all. "I don't care about you at all. Except in the context of what you mean to our baby. Even if we were to marry we would continue to conduct our lives separately."

"I don't want to marry you."

"I did not say I *wanted* to marry you," he said, taking a seat across from her. "Only that I feel it is an option."

She studied him hard. "You believe me. About the baby?"

"Yes."

"And you want the baby. You want to be a father."

"I am going to be a father. That means I…have to be one," he said, sounding slightly less confident than he typically did.

"Why did you change your mind?"

"I lived in Rome when I was a boy." He leaned back in his chair and picked up his glass of wine, swirling the liquid inside slowly. "We lived in a very poor neighborhood. I never knew my father. I woke up one morning and the house was empty. Everything had been taken. And there were strangers there. My mother was gone. And I kept asking them where she was, but no one would answer me. I found out later that she was killed on her way home from work. I assume the landlord took all of our possessions and left me alone. But I don't know the details, and things like that are always difficult to sort through. Childhood memories. The recollections of a five-year-old are not always clear. But I know what it means to be alone. I know what it is like to feel lost." There was a faraway look in his dark eyes, a deep well that she could not see the bottom of. So different to the flatness that was usually there. "I do not wish that for our child. I wish for them to have a full house. I wish for them to have both of us. If he wakes in the middle of the night I do not want him to be alone."

Her chest tightened to the point of discomfort. She looked down at her plate, picked up an olive and rolled it in between her thumb and forefinger. Emotions made her uncomfortable. Especially the emotions of other people. In her experience connecting was dangerous. Empathy was dangerous. It had made it impossible to do what her father asked growing up. Because if she started to think too deeply about what other people would feel when they discovered they had been cheated, she had to contend with her conscience.

And if ever she connected with people, it only dissolved once the con ended and she had to run.

It was why she could never engage herself. Why she had to play a character wholly and completely, so that she was wrapped in it, so the real her was protected.

But she found that she was not protected now. She was not distant. Because it was too easy to picture a lonely boy in an empty house. Because she had felt that, too.

"Some nights," she said, questioning the words even as she spoke them, "my father would go to events, and he could not bring me with him. He would tell me to lock the doors, not open them for anyone. We had a password. So when he came home in the early hours of the morning, he would say it, and I would know not to be afraid. But sometimes he didn't come home. And I would be by myself all night. Normally I would sleep through it, but sometimes I would wake up, go get a glass of water, something like that. And the house was so empty. It's a very scary feeling late at night." She met his gaze. "I don't want that for our child, either. I want what you want."

Her stomach twisted hard. She didn't really want to deal with him, because he frightened her. Because he had used her. Because he had scraped away the layers of rock she kept between herself and the world, made her vulnerable to him. Exposed her to him. She could not forget that.

"He will have it," Rocco said, a certainty in his voice that she found oddly comforting. "It is a terrifying thing as a child. Being alone in that way. I am...sorry that you were alone. I know that feeling. It is... I avoid it at all costs now."

She swallowed hard, an unexpected wave of emotion washing over her. "Thank you."

Then, as though he had not just softened for her, he straightened, his eyes unreadable again. "Then it is settled. We are staying here for the foreseeable future."

"Why?" Her heart was pounding fast, fluttering in her chest like a panicked bird.

"Because I don't trust you. I do not trust that you will not find a way to make off with my money and my baby. Your word has limited value to me."

His words cut close to the bone, because there was so much truth to them. Because initially she had intended to take his money and go. Because she was a liar, and she had proven herself to be. And she could not even find a shred of righteous indignation to throw back at him. "I am being honest with you," she said. It was all she could say.

He looked at her, his gaze hard. "I cannot read you, and I find that disturbing. Are you a practiced con woman? Are you an innocent virgin? Are you a tough girl from the wrong side of the tracks forced into criminal activity because of your circumstances and your upbringing? I don't know. Because I have seen you play all those roles. And you play them all very well."

"Maybe I'm all of them." She reached down and put her fingers on her water glass, turning it in a circle. "And what about you? Who are you? A lonely boy without a mother? The wicked predator who blackmailed me into bed?"

"I am definitely the second. I decided long ago to move past where I began. Feeling guilty doesn't benefit you, Charity. You make decisions—you must own them."

"So, you don't think I should feel guilty about the money my father took and the part I played in it?"

He took a sip of his wine. "If I were you? I wouldn't feel guilty in the least. However, I am not you. I am me, and I had to ensure that you paid for what you did."

"With sex."

"I already told you," he said, his eyes meeting hers. "That was not part of the plan."

"And I already told you I don't trust people. I'm not sure why you think I should take you at your word."

"Because I have no reason to lie to you. Not on that score."

Charity laughed and took a piece of bread from the basket at the center of the table. "Who is going to teach our child morals? It seems that you and I both lack them."

How was she supposed to teach a child right and wrong? How was she supposed to enforce consequences for wrong behavior when she'd spent so much of her life dodging consequences.

When she'd been a thief for so long.

For the first time she wondered if she deserved to go to prison. She didn't want to. But she was guilty of all she was accused of.

She clenched her hands into fists, a sick feeling settling in the pit of her stomach. She couldn't go to jail. Then her child wouldn't have a mother.

She could be better, though. Something was changing in her. For the first time she didn't just *know* that stealing from him was wrong. She *felt* it.

Rocco frowned. "We should get a nanny."

Charity was about to disagree, but then realized he was probably right. She didn't know the first thing about babies, after all. Someone was going to have to show her how to change a diaper.

"We...we probably should."

"We will worry about that a little bit later. For now, I suggest we get used to dealing with each other."

"Do we have to?" she asked, picking up her glass of water. "We could always just ignore each other."

"I would much rather sleep with you again."

She sputtered. "What?"

"Why not? We are attracted to one another. And you will be here indefinitely. It could benefit us both."

"Yeah. No." She picked up another piece of bread and ate it. "I spend most days feeling a lot like I just licked the underside of a shoe. So I can honestly tell you that sex is the furthest thing from my mind. In fact, I'm a little bit angry at sex. I blame sex."

He shrugged, looking completely unconcerned by her refusal. "Fair enough."

She was slightly wounded that he didn't press. Which was ridiculous. She should not be wounded. She should be thrilled. Or something. She didn't want to sleep with him again. He hated her. He had only brought her here because she was having his baby.

Come to that, *she* wasn't that fond of *him*.

Yes, in that hotel suite, in the heat of the moment, with a veil of fantasy drawn around them that had begun with that note and that lingerie, something had caught fire between them. But here, with the brine from the ocean playing havoc with her sensitive stomach, the cool breeze blowing across her skin, raising goose bumps on her arms, things felt all too real.

Still, the rejection stung a little bit, even if she didn't know why. Some sort of previously unknown feminine sexual pride that had been uncovered by their indiscretion.

Just another bit of evidence to prove that sleeping with him in the first place was incredibly stupid.

"So that's it then?"

"Did you think I was going to pine after you?" He looked her over, his dark eyes conveying a kind of dismissiveness that cut deep. "I'm used to much more experienced women, *cara mia*, and while your innocence had a certain charm I prefer a partner who understands the way a man's body works."

Heat assaulted her cheeks. "You were the one who propositioned me."

"Because it made sense. I'm not a man prepared to go without sex. I'm hardly going to be celibate, so the decision is yours. Either I sleep with you or I will find someone else."

A ball of rage lodged itself in her chest. She couldn't quite work out why. She had refused him, so, by that logic, he should be free to share his body with whoever he wanted. But she didn't feel that he should be. His body belonged to her. At least, that was what it felt like. He was the only man she had ever touched like that. The only man who had ever been inside her. How could that not feel significant to him? It didn't seem fair.

But she would not show him her feelings. She would not reveal herself. "Do what you want. I'm not bothered. Just don't touch me."

"I always do what I want. But your gesture of offering permission was cute." He stood, picking up his glass of wine and swallowing the rest of the contents before setting it back on the table. "And on that note, I believe I will go out and do what I please. Have a good evening."

He turned and walked off the terrace, leaving her sitting there. Alone.

She picked up another piece of bread and bit into it with no small amount of ferocity. She didn't care what he went to do. She did not own him. She did not own his body, in spite of her earlier thoughts on the subject.

She didn't want to go out. She wanted to sit here. And eat. Go to bed early.

Master of the Manor aside, the house was beautiful, and she should just enjoy being here. The money her father had stolen would never gain him admittance into a place like this. To a man like Rocco a million dollars was a drop in an endless sea.

So, she would sit here and enjoy the fact that, although her father had abandoned her and left her to take the fall, she was the one sitting in a villa in Italy.

With a man who had blackmailed her into bed. And had got her pregnant. And was headed out to undoubtedly have sex with another woman.

So, except for all those things, she would sit here and enjoy the fact that she was in an Italian villa. She would ignore the other things. For as long as she could.

CHAPTER SIX

ROCCO WRENCHED HIS tie off and cast it down to the marble floor in the entryway of his home. He had gone out, and he had stayed out all night. He had found a beautiful woman, and he had bought her a drink. However, when it had come time for him to take the beautiful woman to bed, he had changed his mind. He had not even kissed her, not even tried to seduce her. He had bought her a drink, chatted with her and realized that his body had no interest in her.

He wasn't entirely certain what to do with that realization. She was a beautiful woman, and there was no reason for him to do anything but take her to bed. However, he found he simply lacked the desire. And so he had spent the rest of the night drinking, attempting to get himself into a place where he might not be so aware of the woman he wanted to seduce. But still, as he had approached a blonde later in the night, Charity—her dark curls, beautifully smooth skin, like coffee and cream—swam before his vision, the pale beauty before him washing out into insignificance.

He had ended his time out as the sky began to turn gray, the sun preparing to rise over the sea, walking through the city using the frigid early-morning air to help sober him up.

And then he had walked back to the villa. He would send someone for his car later.

But, though his head was clear, he was not in a better mood.

He did not understand why he had been immune to those women.

He started up the stairs, unbuttoning the top couple of buttons on his shirt, and the cuffs, pushing the sleeves up to his elbows.

As he made his way down the hall toward his bedroom he heard a thump and a groan.

He paused, turning in the direction of the sound. It was coming from Charity's room.

He did not stop and think; rather he charged toward the door and pushed it open, just in time to see her crawling on all fours into the bathroom. He frowned and strode across the room. In the bathroom, he saw her kneeling in front of the toilet, retching.

He walked in behind her, lifting her hair from her face, until she was finished being sick.

"Go away," she said, her voice pitiful.

"No, I will not go away. You are ill."

"I'm not," she said, sputtering, before leaning back over and being sick again. He made sure her dark curls were pulled away from her face, his fingers making contact with the clammy skin on her forehead, the back of her neck.

"Yes, you are." She slumped backward, her limbs shaking, a shiver racking her frame. "Are you finished?" he asked.

She nodded feebly, and he scooped her up into his arms, conscious of how cool her skin felt, even though it was beaded with perspiration. "Water," she said.

"Of course, but let me get you back into your bed."

"You getting me into bed is what caused this in the first place," she mumbled.

"This is because of the pregnancy?" He set her down at the center of the bed, debating whether or not he should put a blanket over her.

"Well, it isn't food poisoning."

"I have no experience with pregnant women," he said, feeling defensive. "I knew that pregnancy could make you ill, but I did not realize how severe it might be."

She drew her knees up to her chest, curling into a little miserable ball. "Mine is quite severe."

"You seemed well yesterday."

"It usually only does this in the morning."

"Are you cold?"

She shivered. "No, I'm hot."

"You are shivering."

"Okay, now I'm cold."

Rocco didn't know the first thing about caring for another person. He had never done it before. Since the death of his mother he had spent his life renting out connections. Foster families that never kept him for longer than a couple of months, lovers who lasted a couple of nights. In his experience, the only thing that was permanent were the things he could buy. So he invested in things. In brick, and marble. In cars and land. People were too transient in nature. Too temporary.

He remembered—a hazy image—that when he had been ill as a child his mother used to bring him a drink. With a lemon. Or maybe it wasn't a real memory at all. Maybe it was just something his mind had given him, something he had created for his mother's image to replace the more concrete memories of her looking desolate, tired.

Either way, he imagined Charity might like tea.

* * *

Charity watched as Rocco turned wordlessly and walked out of the room. She hadn't really expected him to leave without a word, but all things considered she was relieved. Having him walk in while she was throwing up had to be one of the most humiliating experiences of her life. Vomiting was bad enough. Vomiting in front of Rocco was even worse.

She did not want him seeing her when she was so low. He didn't deserve it.

She crawled to the head of the bed and slipped beneath the covers, exhaustion rolling over her in a wave.

Dimly, she registered that he was wearing the suit he had been wearing last night, though he did not have his tie or jacket on. So that meant he had gone out all night. Very likely, he had slept with someone else.

Misery joined the exhaustion, and she shivered. At least when he'd come into the bathroom he hadn't been cruel. He'd held her hair. Had carried her to bed. It had almost been as if he cared about her comfort.

Which was silly. Because he didn't care about anything. Least of all her.

A few moments later, Rocco reappeared, carrying a tray, his black hair disheveled, his shirt open at the collar, revealing a wedge of tan skin and dark chest hair. His sleeves were rolled up past his elbows, the weight of the tray enhancing the muscles of his forearms. And the strength of his hands.

He really did have wonderful hands.

She liked his hands much better than she liked his mouth, though that was beautiful, too. His hands had only given her pleasure. His mouth did a lot to administer pain.

"What are you doing?" she asked, as he set the tray, which she now saw had a teapot, a cup, a small plate with toast and a little jar of jam, down on the bed.

"This is what you do when people aren't feeling well. Isn't it?"

"Well, it can't hurt." She readjusted herself so that she was sitting, leaning back against the nest of pillows that were on the bed, and the headboard.

Rocco picked up the teapot and the cup, pouring a generous amount for her before handing it to her. "Careful," he said, the warning strange and stilted on his lips, "it's hot."

She lifted the cup to her lips and blew on it gently, before looking over the rim at her delivery service. "Why are you being so nice to me?"

He cleared his throat, a wrinkle appearing between his brows. "I'm not being nice. I am being practical. It does not benefit either of us for you to die."

She sighed heavily into the sip of her tea. "I don't know. If I died you wouldn't have to deal with any of this. You wouldn't have to face fatherhood."

His expression turned grim. "I have dealt with quite enough loss, thank you. I should like to keep you alive. And the baby."

She looked into her tea. "Sorry. That was gallows humor at its worst."

"I think you believe I'm a bit more of a monster that I really am." He said the words slowly, cautiously.

"Probably. But can you blame me, considering our introduction?"

"Can you blame *me*, considering our introduction?" His dark gaze was level, serious. And that guilt, that newfound guilt she felt deep down, bit her.

"I suppose not." She didn't really know what to say to that. Because she couldn't justify her actions, not anymore. She had spent a lot of years doing just that. Because from the cradle, her father had educated her in an alternate morality that was not easy to shake. But the older she got, the more difficult it had become to justify what she knew was stealing.

It had been easy to hold on to righteous indignation where Rocco was concerned because of what had happened between them.

"I'm sorry," she said, before she could fully think it through.

"Why are you apologizing?" he asked, his lips thinning into a grim line.

"Because we stole from you. It was wrong. You can dress things up...you can call them cons. You can call your victims marks. You can pretend it's okay because they have money and you don't. But at the end of the day it is stealing. And regardless of the fact that there was a time when I truly didn't know better, I do now. But...if you knew my father, you would understand how easy it is to get sucked into his plans. There is a reason he is able to talk people into parting with their money, Rocco. He's very convincing. He has a way of making you think everything will be okay. He has a way of making you think that somehow, you deserve what it is you're going after. Regardless, my involvement was wrong. And I'm sorry."

Hopefully, he wouldn't have her thrown in jail.

But she felt that these things had to be said before they could move forward. Or maybe she was just half-delirious because she still didn't feel very well. Or maybe his little gesture with the tea had meant a little bit more than she should let it. Either way, here she was. Confessing.

And she wasn't just confessing to him, but to herself.

Suddenly, she felt drained. Dirty. Desolate.

Acquiring a moral compass was overrated.

"Do you suppose there's a place in life where you become past the point of redemption?" she asked.

"I've never considered it." He sat down on the edge of the bed. "But then, that could be because I never imagined I had the option of redemption."

"I probably don't either then."

"Is it so important? What's the purpose, anyway? Is it that you want to be considered *good*?" he asked.

"I...I never really thought very much about whether or not I was good or bad. I remember asking my father one time why we were afraid of the good guys. The police. Because, even I knew from watching TV that they were supposed to be good. And people who ran from them were bad. So, I asked him if we were bad. He said it isn't that simple. He said sometimes good people do bad things, and bad people do good things. He said that not everyone in a uniform is good. But I just wanted to know if we were good. Maybe I still do."

"Does it matter?"

"Doesn't it? I don't know that anybody aspires to be one of the bad guys. And...I want to teach our child to be good so...I should be, too."

"I suppose you can only really be a good or bad guy in your own life, at least, in my experience. There are a great many people who would characterize me as a villain, though I have never broken the law. However, I have accomplished what I set out to accomplish. I have created the life for myself that I always wanted. What does being good have to do with any of that?"

Charity frowned. "I don't know. But I'm not sure I really know who I am. How can I know if I'm good or bad if I don't know the answer to such a simple question?"

"Do you suppose if we get a nanny she can help us with these sorts of questions?"

Charity laughed, in spite of herself. "You mean, do you

suppose she would mind helping a couple of emotionally stunted adults?"

"I suppose you and I don't make the most functional pair."

"Are we a pair?"

"Only in the sense that there are two of us, and we will be raising this child. Though, in what capacity I'm still not certain."

She wanted to ask him about last night. Wanted to ask him if he had slept with someone else. But it seemed strange, and not her business. Since she had made a grand declaration about the fact that she would not be sleeping with him again.

Though, right now she felt less resolute in that. Possibly because she felt less resolute about everything. Because as soon as she had spoken the words about not knowing who she was, she realized that they were true. She knew how to put on masks, how to play parts. Even when she had decided to step away from her father, from the con games, all she had done was put on the mask of waitress, woman in her early twenties. She hadn't made real connections with anyone, hadn't made friends. Had not assigned any kind of depth to the persona she had been playing for the past couple of years.

For a moment, she was worried that was all there was. That she had played too many parts on too shallow a level to ever find anything beneath them. What kind of mother would that make her? What did that mean for the rest of her life?

No wonder it had been so easy for her mother to leave her. No wonder it had been so easy for her father to detach from her in the end. There was no substance in her to hold on to.

That can't be true.

At least, she wouldn't let it continue to be true. And she'd…she'd felt the implications of what she'd done. She still did. That had to mean something.

She needed dreams. She hadn't let herself have any, not since the last con. Because, she was afraid that her dreams would outstrip her means, and that she would fall back into the same behavior she'd been raised in. But she couldn't live like that. For the sake of her child, she had to be more.

Of course, she had no idea what her future held, because it seemed as though Rocco was currently clutching it in his palm. For those brief moments outside of his office, back in New York, she had imagined a life blissfully raising her child, alone. That had seemed satisfactory. But once again everything had been uprooted. Her fantasies proving impossible.

"Don't worry about whether or not you are good or bad," he said, finally. "What you really need to focus on is making it to a day where you don't vomit in the morning."

"Oh, Rocco. You do fill a girl with hope and butterflies."

He frowned. "I am trying to help."

"But you aren't being nice," she said, a small smile curving her lips. "According to you."

He shook his head. "No, I am being practical. My mother used to bring me tea."

Charity's chest tightened. Imagining Rocco as a little boy, a little boy she knew had ended up alone. It made her ache for him. And it made her feel swollen with emotion. Because, this one bit of tenderness he seemed to know, he had chosen to pass on to her. Whether he called it practicality or kindness, it didn't change the fact that he was giving some to her.

"Well, I appreciate it. I really do." She cleared her throat and picked up one of the pieces of toast, neglecting the jam, because she wasn't certain her stomach could handle it yet. "Though, you don't need to come and hold my hair when I'm… It's gross."

"I find nothing gross about it. You are sick. You are sick because of my baby. It seems only fair that I should take care of you."

"Is that what this is? You're going to take care of me?"

"I confess, I hadn't really thought it through."

"Somehow, I feel like that's the story of every single interaction you and I have had, indirectly or directly," she said.

"Probably. Had one of us been thinking more clearly at any stage of this, things could've turned out quite differently."

"Yes, we should begin that soon."

"I'm thinking quite clearly now."

Charity opened the small jar of jam and began to spread a little bit onto the piece of toast, feeling slightly more emboldened as she had taken three or four bites and not felt her stomach turn once. She lifted the toast to her lips, a little bit of bread crumb getting on her thumb, sticking to where some jam had made contact with her skin.

"I'm glad to hear it," she said.

Silence settled between them and she looked up at him, meeting his eyes. He was watching her, a strange softness in his expression. At least, if it had been any other man she might have thought it was softness. With Rocco, it never was.

"What?" she asked.

"I'm thinking," he said.

"About?"

"The fact that I will probably try and seduce you."

She sputtered, putting her toast back down on the plate, crumbs still sticking to her fingers. "I'm sorry, what?"

"I'm going to seduce you," he said, his tone decisive. "I will succeed. We both know that."

She spread her hands wide. "I just threw up in front of you, and I'm now lying in bed covered in jam. How could you possibly be thinking about seduction? And you really think I'll agree to…be seduced?"

"Yes," he said, turning away and walking toward the door.

"Where are you going?"

"I thought I would wait to seduce you until you felt better. Do you require anything else?"

She felt as if she'd been hit over the head with something very heavy. "No."

"You seem confused."

"How did we get from tea and toast to…seduction?"

"I want you," he said. "I have, from the first moment I saw you. I am…used to having what I want."

"But I'm a woman and not a Ferrari. So you can't just come down to the lot and plunk down cash. I have a say."

"I know," he said. "And I want you to say yes. I value the yes, Charity. It means nothing if you don't want me, too. Which is why I plan to seduce you, not simply take you. We will talk later." Then he stood and walked out, leaving her with a promised seduction, tea and toast.

Seduction really was the most logical course of action. Because he had not been able to force himself to get excited about any of the women he had encountered last night. And he needed to prove to himself that he could take control of whatever this thing was that seemed to take him over whenever he was around Charity.

And when he'd been sitting there, looking down at her he had felt…a strange warmth in his chest. And it had pulled at him. Called to him. And she had asked "what."

What he was thinking, he assumed, and his mind had been blank.

He hadn't been thinking. He'd been feeling.

Then for some reason seduction was the first thing that came out of his mouth.

But really, it made sense.

That day in the hotel she had challenged everything he had ever known about himself. He did not lose control, and yet, with her he had. So he could continue to avoid her, which would keep her in possession of his control, or he could stoke the fire of the things that burned between them, bring them under his command.

Yes, that was definitely the better idea.

The only other option was allowing his beautiful little thief to claim total control over his libido and that was not acceptable.

He strode through the villa, wearing a different suit to the one he had been wearing last night, feeling reinvigorated. He had not slept at all since coming home, but in lieu of sleep, his new plan would do just as well.

He moved through the living area and onto the terrace, taking in the grounds. He had not encountered Charity in the house, and he wondered if she was still sick in bed. Her feeling sick would be an impediment to his plan.

His plan had begun to seem very important, as he doubted he would find another means to get his interactions with her on track. Not as long as he was distracted by his desire for her body.

He could nearly taste her again. Those sweet, dusky-rose lips and the honey between her thighs. He was hard just thinking about it. How long had it been since he'd wanted one woman specifically? Had he ever?

He wanted sex, women in a general sense, but never specifically. Art, cars, *things*, he craved with a ferocious specificity, but never women. He craved *beauty* so that he could collect it, keep it.

He craved things because the more he owned, the more there was of him. The more evidence there was of his power. Never had he felt more helpless than as a boy with nothing. And so, he had become a man with everything.

It was why he had built a house into a carved mountainside that gazed out at the sea, owning a piece of what was wild. Taming it.

He wanted to tame her. Keep her. Make her his.

The epiphany was utterly disturbing, and yet he realized, standing there scanning all that he owned, it was her he was searching for. And no amount of awareness about the nature of his attraction would stop him searching for her.

She had him. And he had to reverse that ownership.

He saw a faint splash coming from the courtyard, from the large infinity pool that overlooked the sea. His gut tightened. It was her. He knew it was her.

He moved away from the terrace and back into the living room, striding out the double doors that led to the walled-in garden. There was an outdoor living area, with a bed and gauzy curtains, perfect for those times when he simply couldn't wait to get a lover indoors. The pool and its glass wall faced the sea and a completely private beach, if he enjoyed the feeling of putting on a show without actually having an audience.

And Rocco had to confess, without any shame, that he did.

He looked at the pool and saw barely a ripple. Then, her sleek, dark head resurfaced. She had her back to him, her black curls tamed by the water. She pushed her hands back over her hair, droplets sluicing down over her hair, her arms.

"The view from here is very nice," he said.

She whirled around quickly, her eyes wide, her mouth open. His eyes fell to the low cut of the bathing suit she was wearing—one that must have been provided by his staff, as he had requested sometime last night that they see to it that his guest had clothes. It was a one-piece suit. Out of deference to her pregnancy, he imagined. And yet it was still incredibly sexy.

He couldn't tear his eyes away from her breasts. They were average size, he supposed, but incredible. Perfectly round with lovely, caramel nipples that had set his body on fire. He was obsessed with tasting her again. Everywhere.

"I thought so," she said, offering him a strained smile. "You picked a great location for the pool."

"I wasn't talking about the ocean."

Her cheeks darkened. "Oh."

He moved closer to the pool, closer to her. He couldn't help himself.

With her, he could never seem to help himself. "You are beautiful, *cara mia*, surely you know that."

She lifted a shoulder, a water droplet rolling down her skin. "I don't think about it often."

"Not at all?"

She shrugged again and began to walk toward the steps of the pool. Slowly she rose from the water, revealing her body inch by delectable inch. He could not yet see any changes from the pregnancy, though she was nearly at the three-month mark by now. She was still slim, the rounded curves of her body pure perfection. He could remember clearly what it had been like to run his hands over all that bare skin…

"It doesn't mean anything to me. In my position in life either you use your beauty to manipulate, or you don't. Until I met you, I'd never used my body. Not even for a con."

"I am curious," he said, and he found he was, "when did you stop helping your father? And why did you go back?"

She let out a heavy sigh and walked over to the chair that had a white towel folded and placed in the center. She picked it up and started to dry herself, wrapping it tightly around her hips. "When I was about seventeen I told him I didn't want to play the game anymore. He wasn't happy, but I was basically taking care of myself anyway. A lot of what I did was facilitating corporate scams and charity frauds." She lowered her eyes. "It was bad. But I'd always done it and…I just didn't think much about it. He used to say that there was no amount of hard work that could ever get regular people like us to the top. He said if people weren't smart enough they didn't deserve to keep their cash. 'A fool and his money are soon parted' was always one of his favorite phrases. Of course, it never applied to him and how fast he went through whatever he got."

"Naturally not," Rocco said, keeping his voice neutral.

"But there was a point when I realized it was…not something I wanted to do. So I stopped. And he left town about six months later. I got a job waitressing. I'd been doing that for about three years when he came back. I hadn't heard from him at all for the last year. And I was struggling and it sounded so easy. More than that…my dad was back. I've never been able to say no to him because I just want to be…I want us to be a family. He's all I have. And it was just one more job—hit AmariCorp, get them to invest in us, roll out with the money. I swear I didn't know it would be so much. And…look, it was wrong," she said, dark eyes blazing, "I know it was. Old habits and stuff. I got tempted to cut corners and I didn't hold up to the temptation. I did it because I knew that I wouldn't make that much in a year of work and I was tired of struggling. And then he took off, and I felt like crap and I just…well,

I never saw any of the money we took from you. It took us a couple months to organize the scam, another one for me to realize my dad left me in the lurch and another three for you to find me. And you made me pay, Rocco. You made me pay enough that I know I'll remember the cost if I'm ever tempted again. Nothing is free."

Her words sat uncomfortably in his gut. "I made you pay. With sex?"

"Among other things. I don't know if I ever truly understood how wrong it all was until I met you and it…it hurts."

"I feel I have asked too much of you," he said, moving to close the distance between them. "I am…I regret the way things passed between us."

"You're sorry?" she asked, tilting her head to the side.

He frowned. "I would not go that far."

"I feel all warm inside, Rocco. I really do."

He moved to her, wrapped his arm around her waist and tugged her up against his body. His heart was raging, his hands shaking and he didn't have any idea why.

"I am not sorry," he said, his voice rough, "because I cannot regret wanting you. I cannot regret having you. Even though I should."

He raised his hand to her cheek and slid his thumb over her lip, slicking up a drop of water that remained there. She was the epitome of beauty, a living embodiment of all the things he surrounded himself with. All the things he tried to collect. All of the things he wanted to own. And she didn't want him.

It enraged him, that she was so close to him, and yet so far from him in so many ways.

No, it was unacceptable. He would not endure it.

"I'm cold," she said, shivering.

"I could make you warm," he said, his voice rough.

"Why?" she asked, her eyes searching his.

"Because I want you," he said, tracing the perfectly shaped line of her upper lip before sliding his fingertips over her sculpted cheekbones. Learning her face. Taking possession of it.

"But I don't understand *why* you want me. You've given me every indication that you hate me. You humiliated me in New York. You used me. And whether you want to talk about it or not, you paid for my body. It doesn't make sense."

"None of this makes sense. When you walked into that hotel in New York I had every intention of humiliating you. I wanted to leave you in that hotel room aching and begging for me. I didn't think I would want you. How could I want a thief?" He gripped her chin between his thumb and forefinger. "I don't think you understand, Charity. Nobody steals from me. What I have earned is precious to me in ways very few people comprehend. I despised you before I laid eyes on you. I was not supposed to want you."

"So why do you?"

"There is no reason. Except for chemistry. This is truly potent chemistry, *cara*, and I certainly don't know how to fight it. The fact is, I don't want to. I spent many years deprived of human contact, living with families who showed me no affection. I spent a great many years without the things that I truly craved. And I do not believe in denying myself, not now. Now I have the power to deliver to myself everything I desire. I have no practice at it and restraint. And no need for it. And so I underestimate you, and where the attraction to you would lead. And now I find that I'm aware of how powerful it is, I want to explore it."

"I don't see why I should sleep with a man who despises me."

"You did it once."

She looked down, her expression stricken. "I'm not proud of it."

"Why?" He tightened his grip on her chin, forcing her to look back at him. "Why aren't you proud? You nearly brought me to my knees. You made me weak with wanting. You forced me to deviate from my plan, and no one does that, Charity, *no one*. You could bring me to my knees now if you would promise to let me taste the beauty between your thighs. How can you not feel some pride in that?"

"I suppose," she said, her voice trembling, her cheeks flooded with dark color, "I suppose it's because I have never put much stock in sexual attraction. I've never really felt that before you, not in a specific sense."

"Sex drives the world. There is very little that is more powerful." He laughed, though he didn't feel anything was particularly funny. "Perhaps money. And our interactions have been fueled by both. Is it any wonder we are so potent together?"

"I don't want this," she said, her voice a whisper.

"You don't want my attentions? Or you don't want to feel this attraction?"

"I don't want to feel this," she said, not looking at him.

"But you do," he said, his voice fierce. "You do."

"Yes."

"I do not despise you," he said, the words a rough whisper. "I recognize something in you."

"What?" she asked.

"Hunger. You are so empty. So hungry. Like me." She nodded, emotion flashing bright in her dark eyes. "Let me fill you."

She nodded and it was all the consent he needed.

He dipped his head and captured her lips, a raw sound rumbling in his chest as he did, the relief that flooded him unlike anything he had ever known. He was so hungry for this, so hungry for her, and he had not realized until the taste of her dropped onto his tongue. Only then did he realize just how intense the craving was.

He coaxed her mouth open, sliding his tongue against hers, tasting her deeply, drinking her in as he would do a fine brandy, savoring her, letting the heat flood every part of him, warming the deep places that were always cold.

But she went deeper than any alcohol could ever burn, touching a part of his soul he had not realized still lived.

Wanting her became the physical ache, a drive that he could not fight, a drive he did not want to fight.

She was far too stiff in his arms for his liking. He slid his hand down to the curve of her bottom, pulling her tightly against him, against his growing arousal, showing her exactly how she affected him, exactly how much he wanted her. And she began to soften in his arms, a sound of capitulation on her lips, as she tasted him as deeply as he had been tasting her. As she allowed herself to get drunk on him, as he had been doing on her. And he felt her grow languid, felt her melt against him, her breasts pressed against his chest, an eroticism he didn't think he had ever fully paused to appreciate before.

He was a jaded man, a man with too much experience. Kisses had long since ceased to thrill him. But this kiss was everything. It was more than any kiss. More than he had ever imagined a kiss could be.

"I must have you," he said, wrenching his mouth from hers so that he could speak the words that were burning in his chest. "I need you, Charity, I need you."

It vexed him, even now, that she could make him want so deeply. With all of himself. This little thief who had reached inside of him and stolen the very thing he prized the most: his control.

Right now, he was not even certain if he wanted it back. The only thing he was certain of wanting was her.

He gripped the straps to her swimsuit, pulling them down her arms and revealing her breasts. He lowered his head, taking one nipple into his mouth, sucking her in deeply and groaning as he relished the taste of her. She was everything, everything he had remembered and more.

"We shouldn't do this," she said, breathless, as lost as he was.

He traced the shape of her with the tip of his tongue reveling in the difference in texture between her creamy skin and the tightened bud. "We shouldn't," he said, breathing hard. "We absolutely should not. But you and I are notorious for doing things we shouldn't. I see no reason to change now. Not when this feels so good."

She said nothing, but she wove her fingers through his hair, held him to her as he continued to indulge his craving for her. He shaped her curves with his palms, absorbing every bit of her softness, committing this to memory. In case this was the last time. Because he would take nothing for granted with her, ever. He could not predict her, and in his life finding something so unpredictable was rare. He enjoyed it as much as he feared it. Another rarity.

He rolled her wet suit down her hips, and she stepped out of it, kicking it to the side. He raised his head and kissed her lips deeply again, before turning around so that she was facing away from him, wrapping her hair around his hand and pressing down gently on her shoulders with his other hand, so that she was leaning over the outdoor sofa.

He traced the elegant line of her spine with the tip of his finger, all the way down, until he was teasing the damp entrance to her body, testing her readiness. She was wet,

wet and ready for him. He leaned in, pressing a kiss to the back of her neck, and she shivered beneath his touch.

He freed himself from the confines of his trousers and positioned himself at her damp core, bracing himself by holding more tightly to her hair, and gripping her hip, as he sank into her softness slowly. She tugged against his hold, turning her head so that her eyes met his, her lips parted, her eyes wide. He flexed his hips forward so that he was buried inside of her to the hilt, and a raw sound escaped her mouth.

"Good?" he asked, the word strained.

She nodded slightly, encountering resistance thanks to the tight restraints he'd placed on her. He withdrew slightly, before thrusting back home, establishing a steady rhythm designed to drive them both to the brink. He slipped his hand forward, placing it between her thighs, teasing her clitoris with his movements.

Release started to build in him, far too soon—he wanted this to last, wanted her screaming his name before he took his own pleasure. He gritted his teeth, increased the pressure on the bundle of nerves he was focused on. He heard her gasp, and he took it as approval. He continued to tease her, pushing her closer and closer. Could feel her internal muscles tightening around him, could feel the climax building inside of her. He leaned forward, still stroking her, and grazed the side of her neck with his teeth. A hoarse cry escaped her lips and she dropped over the edge.

And then he stopped holding back. He pounded into her heat, chasing his own release, his blood roaring in his ears as he came hard, the sound of his own release mingling with hers.

When the storm subsided, he moved away from her, breathing hard. The outline of his fingers red on her hip, the evidence of his passion left in the slight impressions on the delicate skin of her neck, stood out like beacons in the night, irrefutable proof of his lack of control. And yet, he could not bring himself to regret it.

She was trembling, and he swept her up into his arms, an echo of their first time together back in New York. But this time, he would not be leaving her. This time, she would spend the night in his bed. With him.

CHAPTER SEVEN

CHARITY ROLLED ONTO her back and stretched, raising her hands above her head, her knuckles cracking against the hardwood headboard. A headboard she did not have at her apartment in Brooklyn.

She opened her eyes and looked around the room. Late-afternoon sunlight was filtering through gauzy white curtains. Because she wasn't in Brooklyn, she was in Rocco's villa. Though, the late-afternoon sunlight was a little bit more confusing.

She sat upright, the sheet falling down to her waist. She was naked. She supposed she shouldn't be surprised.

Then a host of images filtered through her mind, memories of the way they had spent the majority of the day. And she *knew* she shouldn't be surprised by her nudity.

Just then, Rocco came walking into the room from the bathroom, as naked as she was. And clearly a lot less self-conscious about it.

"So, all of that…happened." She reached down and gripped the edge of the sheet, drawing it back up over her breasts.

A smile curved his lips. "Yes. More than once."

"What time is it?"

"Nearly six."

So they had been in bed all day. Which was one way

to while away the hours when she felt wretched. Have orgasms instead. Really, it was kind of a no-brainer. Climaxes were better than vomiting.

She didn't feel sick at all right now. In fact, she felt hungry. Starving.

"Dinner will be sent up shortly." It was as if he could read her mind. Disconcerting, but handy in this particular situation. And in others.

When it came to what she wanted in bed he seemed to be able to read her mind better than she could. She was so inexperienced that until him she hadn't really known what she might want. But he was showing her. With great skill.

He was every bit as commanding between the sheets as he was out of them. And it turned out she quite liked it.

Less so when they were vertical than when they were horizontal, but they would work on that.

She had no idea what this arrangement between the two of them was supposed to be. They were having a baby. They were, as of a few hours ago, sleeping together. But she was still the woman who had stolen his money, and she doubted that he had forgotten that along the way.

He was still the man who had forced her to come to Italy with him. Still the man who had held the threat of prison over her head, who had sent her that note, and the lingerie.

That hadn't changed. But for some reason, it felt as if the air between them had. Which was silly. People didn't change, not really. They only put on new masks. New costumes. She knew that better than anyone. She had spent her entire life doing it. She had proven it when she'd hopped right back into the con ring the moment her father had shown up and offered her a chance at taking the easy road again.

She'd shed her waitress uniform quickly enough and fallen back into old patterns. She couldn't imagine a future where she wouldn't do it again. No matter how settled she thought she might be.

If she hadn't managed to change before, why would she be able to do it now?

"What sort of dinner?" she asked, because it was an innocuous question, which felt necessary right now. And because she was interested in food.

"I didn't specify. Beyond that it be easy to eat in bed." He crossed the room and sat down on the edge of the mattress, and her stomach turned over, her heart rate increasing. Being close to him again made her want things. Already. Again.

"You don't think we should get up for a while?" she asked.

"I think that sounds like a terrible idea. I would rather stay in here all day." He looked at her, and for once his dark eyes weren't flat. They weren't filled with anger or mockery of any kind. They were warm. And it made her feel warm. A flame that started at the center of her stomach and radiated outward.

He adjusted his position and moved toward her, placing his hands on either side of her as he leaned in for a kiss. It was a brief meeting of their mouths, nothing to get too excited about. And yet, for all that it was so brief it was that much more exciting.

"That seems…decadent."

He arched a brow. "Decadent? An interesting choice of words for a woman such as yourself."

"What's that supposed to mean?"

"I had imagined you had tasted your share of real decadence. Given that…"

She shifted uncomfortably, her throat tightening. "That we stole money."

He slid his thumb over her cheekbone. "I did not mean it like that."

She wasn't sure if she should deflect or opt for a little bit of honesty. Which seemed silly in a lot of ways, as they were sitting here naked with each other. And a certain degree of honesty should be implied by that. But while they had shared their bodies, she wasn't certain they had shared anything deeper than that.

"Sometimes it was like that." The words came out rusty, rough. "When my dad ran a con and things went well, there was a lot of sitting back and enjoying the spoils. Of course I didn't realize that's what I was doing. But you know, we would have weeks of going out to dinner every night. And they sort of made up for the weeks where we hadn't had food at all. Weeks spent with my dad smiling and laughing and…being with me. Yes, that was decadent to me." She looked down at her hands. "As I got older I realized exactly what we were doing. And I struggled with it. But my father is a con man. And he does a good job of spinning a story. He did a good job of spinning one about us. About what we were doing. About how we were just working like anyone else. The people we stole things from were too rich to notice what was missing. And if they did notice, then they deserved it for being stupid enough to let us get hold of it." She repeated her father's words, almost verbatim. He always said them with a smile. As though he were partly joking. As though none of it were real.

Just make-believe. A game. A game that happened to be a crime. A game that happened to be immoral. But a game nonetheless.

"I see," he said, a strange light in his eyes.

"Like I told you. He's small-time. What he did to you is the biggest job he's ever pulled. At least as far as I know. If he has money like that, other than yours of course, stashed anywhere he certainly never told me about it. And considering he seemed more than willing to let me take the fall for this and leave me without money…"

"You truly do not have it."

She shook her head. "I don't. I never did. I helped him get it but…I don't have it."

"I believe you," he said.

Her stomach twisted. "So much for family. So much for decadence, too."

"So would you say I'm your first taste of decadence?" he asked, his voice positively wicked now.

Heat speared her stomach, blooming outward, flooding her cheeks. "You know you're the first man I've been with."

"Yes," he said, his voice rough and gentle at the same time. "And I am intrigued about that. Would you care to elaborate?"

"Well, I had never had sex before. Then I met you. And I had sex with you."

He angled his head and leaned in, biting her lower lip. The sharp shock of pain faded quickly, ending on a sizzling burst of pleasure that flowed through her entire body. "That is not what I meant." There was something that looked a lot like humor in his eyes, and she wasn't really sure what to do with that.

But she liked it.

"Sex seems like an awful lot of stripping. A good con woman doesn't like to remove her masks. I know I don't. So I was never in a hurry to get that close to anyone. I mean, I could have been with someone if I'd wanted to. But I would've been playing a role. And that never sat well with me."

"And with me? With me in the hotel room, back in New York. And with me now? Are you yourself?" He leaned in, pressing a kiss to her jawline. "Or are you still wearing a mask?"

His gaze met hers, his dark eyes boring into hers, and she had to look away. "I don't know. I have no idea who I am. I've spent every day of my life playing a part. Even the waitress…the version of myself that was supposed to be good. Supposed to be honest—that was a role. I was only *pretending* to be normal. Slipping on the costume. But at the end of the day I would take it off and…I just felt like me again. I didn't feel different. I'm always pretending."

"And with me?"

She took a deep breath, her heart thundering hard. "That's what terrifies me most." It was the truth. And she didn't know why she was admitting it. Didn't know why she felt compelled to offer him the kind of honesty she'd rarely even given to herself.

"What? What terrifies you, *cara mia*?"

"That the day we made love in New York was the most honest I've ever been. With myself. With anyone." She swallowed hard. "I'm not sure I liked her." She said the last part slowly, heat assaulting her cheeks.

"And why didn't you like her?"

"Because she…" She was starting to feel stupid talking about herself in the third person. "I…I slept with you. And I didn't even know you. And I liked it."

"And that's a problem?"

She looked down, her voice muted. "For a lot of people, yes, it would be."

"It isn't for me." He shifted his position so that he was sitting next to her. "I spent too many years *wanting* things. So I don't now. I *take*. I *have*. I don't *want*."

"I do. That's pretty much all I do." That was true, too. Another thing she wasn't certain she should've shared.

"Not anymore. Not with me. I can give you anything

you want. I can give our child anything they might want. Anything they might need. And I will do the same for you. I promise, with me it will only ever be feast, Charity. You will never have to live through famine again. I swear it." His voice was fierce, his dark eyes intent on hers. "I can give you decadence. You will never want for it again."

She wanted to take him up on that promise. She wanted to sink into it. To sink into him, to cling to him and make him promise never to let her go.

It was then she remembered that he'd never promised her fidelity. And he had never promised a relationship. He was only promising things.

And he had gone out last night.

He might have slept with someone else less than twenty-four hours ago.

The idea made her skin crawl.

"You went out last night," she said, conscious of the insecurity in her tone.

He paused for a moment, his dark eyes flat. "Yes, I did."

"Did you sleep with someone else?" Her chest tightened painfully.

"No," he said, his tone definitive.

The knot loosened slightly, her heart pounding hard. "Don't lie to me. Not about that."

"I have no reason to. You know that."

"Don't," she said, her voice a whisper. "Don't lie to me. And don't sleep with anyone else."

He put his palm on her cheek, his dark brows drawing together. "Forever, *cara mia*? That's an awfully long time. I doubt either of us can predict the future quite that well."

She couldn't imagine ever wanting another man. But then…she was inexperienced. He was not. She couldn't fathom it now—but maybe someday.

But she doubted it. "Then at least not while you're sing with me."

"I promise," he said, his tone grave.

It was enough for her. It was enough for now. So she leaned in and kissed him, leaning in to his lips, to his promises, to his decadence. Because she was tired of wanting.

And in Rocco there was satisfaction. So she was determined to seize it.

For as long as possible.

Rocco was certain he had left some of his sanity back in that bed. Back beneath the covers with Charity. And for some reason he couldn't bring himself to be disturbed by that.

He had promised her fidelity.

Granted, he didn't think he could make his body respond to another woman even if his brain wanted him to. Hell, he *knew* he couldn't. He had tried. He had failed.

Even so, he didn't promise such things to women. Because he knew they might start thinking that they had a more permanent place in his life than they did. Though, if any woman had a permanent place in his life it was Charity. Not as his lover, certainly, but as the mother of his child.

As his lover… She was incredibly beautiful. Incredibly responsive. And right now he couldn't imagine preferring anyone over her. But sex was all about satisfying the immediate need. And he had no idea how his immediate needs might shift over the course of the next few weeks. He had never practiced long-term commitment. And he didn't intend to start now.

But he would honor his promise. His promise not to take anyone else to bed, as long as she was in it.

He didn't want to hurt her. Which brought him back to his missing sanity.

He couldn't even regret it. She was too beautiful. But it was more than beauty. There were many beautiful women in the world, and he had been with a good percentage of them.

It was everything she was. Her inexperience, combined with her enthusiasm. The smooth perfection of her coffee-colored skin, a confection so sweet he could lick every inch of it and never be satisfied.

He wanted to buy her something. A necklace. He could envision it now. Something with a heavy pendant that would settle in the valley between her breasts. He could picture her wearing that and nothing else.

Damn, he was obsessed.

And he was beginning to think he might want to bring her to the gala he was attending this weekend. He never brought dates to such events. It was a chance to find a woman for a night of fun, not come shackled.

But he was well and truly shackled, so he might as well embrace it. He had always enjoyed showing off his new things, after all.

A new car, a new villa, new suit and tie even. He liked those outward shows of power. Those claims to his new life that couldn't be taken from him. And he liked others to see them.

Perhaps it would do him well to show Charity off, as well. His newest acquisition.

For some reason the idea of it sent a wave of satisfaction through him, a sharp adrenaline rush that always came from adding another thing to his collection. The kind of rush he never experienced over a woman, because sex, while enormously satisfying, was cheap and easy to come by. The woman never mattered, only that he got what he wanted.

Though, Charity mattered. If only because she was the mother of his child. Really, he could not come up with another reason why she should. Unbidden, his thoughts flashed back to the afternoon he'd spent in bed with her. It was difficult to pretend that didn't matter. The taste of her, the scent of her. Every damn thing about her. The way her black curls tumbled over his pillow, as untamed and wild as she was.

Just thinking about her got him hard.

He shifted, adjusting his position at his desk. She had him acting like a schoolboy. It was disturbing. But delicious in its way. If only because he couldn't remember enjoying anything quite so much at any other point in his life.

Yes, he would bring her to the gala. And he would take her out today to find a dress. She said she had had a lack of decadence in her life, and he would see to it that it was rectified.

He would mourn the lost time with her in the bedroom. But she had scarcely been out of the villa since they'd arrived in Italy, and he wanted her to have a chance to experience the beauty of his home country. A smile curved his lips. He would make a private appointment at a boutique in town. That way if he had a desire to remove every gown after she tried them on, they would not be disturbed.

He reached toward his phone, his decision made.

Adrenaline fired through his blood as he thought of what it would be like to walk into the gala with Charity on his arm. A clear and outward sign of his possession. And yes, he did want to possess her. There were a few things he was uncertain about these days, but at the moment that wasn't one of them.

She would be his. On that score there was no uncertainty.

Charity had been surprised by Rocco's abrupt announcement that they were going out. Mainly because every time he had walked into the room over the past couple of days it had ended, not in them going out, but in them getting naked and satisfying their need for each other on the nearest available surface. Not that she was complaining.

It was a strange thing, to have shared so much physically with someone while exchanging so few words. To exchange such deep, intense intimacies without the common intimacies you could simply speak.

Even so, it was more than she had with anyone else in her life. More than she had ever had. And he was doing strange things to her heart, twisting it around, cinching it in tight, making her feel as though she couldn't breathe.

She was surprised when today he hadn't taken her clothes off. He had ushered her into his car instead. And now he was driving them into the heart of the village that was down the mountain from the villa. She had done absolutely no exploring of their surroundings, not since he had driven her up to his home at the beginning of the week.

He maneuvered the car effortlessly through the narrow cobblestone streets, coming to a stop in front of a shop with an unassuming facade. Red brick and the wooden trim all painted in black with a round sign hanging above the door.

"We have an appointment," he said, putting the car in Park and killing the engine before getting out. He rounded to her side of the car and held the door open for her, the show of chivalry unexpected and dangerous to her already-vulnerable heart. A sense of warmth joined the squeezing feeling.

"To do what? You realize that you have been very cagey. Possibly more cagey than I am on a daily basis. And that's saying something."

He smiled, something he was doing with more and more frequency these days. "It's a surprise."

Her stomach tightened, hope mingling with fear. Because things just didn't come through in her life. Surprises had never been anything good. And she was afraid to hope now that they might be.

She didn't understand this relationship she'd found herself in. Didn't understand what was happening to her at this moment in time. But she wasn't even sure if she wanted to. She just wanted to close out the world, the future, the reality, and keep living in it.

"Trust me," he said, extending his hand.

"You know I don't trust anyone," she said, her voice breathless even to her own ears.

"Okay then, right now. Trust me right now."

She reached out and took his hand, and his fingers closed around hers, his grip strong. "I can do that."

He tugged her forward, leading her into the shop. Inside they were greeted by a petite Italian woman dressed all in black, her hair pulled back into a severe bun, her lips painted a bright red.

"Mr. Amari," she said, inclining her head, "I have set aside a few selections based upon your description of both the event and your friend here," she said, gesturing to Charity. Charity was not sure how she felt about being called Rocco's friend in quite that tone. She was not his friend. She was his lover. Though, she imagined the woman meant escort or something. But Charity wasn't that, either.

Are you really his lover, though? What are you really?

She gritted her teeth and met the other woman's eyes, forcing a smile. She was not a shrinking violet. That much she was sure of. If she had one legacy from her father that she would claim and use, it was the ability to shine in any situation, at least outwardly.

"Charity Wyatt," Charity said, extending her hand. "It's nice to meet you."

The shopkeeper was clearly surprised by the introduction, but she took Charity's offered hand and shook it, and Charity could tell she had won a bit of grudging respect.

"If you don't mind," Rocco said, "we will continue to the back to begin trying things on. Now that you have seen Charity, perhaps you have a few other selections to recommend?"

The woman could tell she had been dismissed, but because Rocco was so darn rich and powerful, it was also clear that she wouldn't argue, even though she wanted to. "Of course, Mr. Amari. Everything is set up in the back, and if you need anything at all just let me know."

"We will," Rocco said, tightening his hold on Charity's hand and leading her toward the back of the store, into an alcove that was furnished with plush chairs, a three-way mirror and a little changing area that was partitioned off from the rest of the room by a thick velvet curtain.

"And are you going to tell me what's going on now?" she asked, abruptly realizing that she had no idea what she was doing here.

"I have a gala to attend tomorrow night. I thought you would like to be my guest," he said, sitting down in the chair and sprawling out, his long legs stretched out in front of him, his elbows positioned on the armrest, fingers tented beneath his chin, his gaze watchful.

She blinked. "You've only just decided you want to take me?"

"I never bring women to such events. This is some sort of charity thing—I'm not sure for what. I don't really care. I'll throw money in the box, and it's good for my name."

"Why do you want to bring me?"

He frowned. "What sort of question is that?"

"You don't normally take women to these sorts of

things, you just said. Now you want to take me. And I'm wondering what changed."

"I decided I didn't want to meet a woman at the event and take her home with me. That is the beginning and end of why I don't bring dates to these sorts of things. But you are the only woman I want to go home with, so it stands to reason you should come with me."

Some of the warmth in her chest was squashed by his words. "Oh."

He looked away, as he often did when she started getting personal or emotional. "Were you expecting something else? I am not a sentimental man, *cara mia*. You should have realized that by now. Honest, yes. Sentimental? No. I can fully satisfy your carnal desires, but your finer feelings will have to be dealt with elsewhere. Perhaps watching romantic movies?"

It made her angry that he did that. That he minimized then what had, for a brief, shining moment, become such a large thing in her mind.

A chance to be brought into his world. A chance to be part of it. A part of him.

So she didn't feel so alone.

"You're assuming I have any finer feelings," she said, turning and walking into the dressing room, shutting the velvet curtain behind her. "I'm only a con woman after all. It's very likely I don't have them."

She turned and saw an array of dresses hung there, waiting for her. She was having a flashback to that moment in her apartment, when she had realized that she was caught. When she was staring at a lingerie bag, a dress and a demand.

But this was different. This time, she had her choice of dress.

She reached out and touched the hem of one of the

gowns, the fabric soft, finer than anything she could have afforded under normal circumstances. She touched each one of them, settling on the one in emerald green, the softest to the touch.

"I never said you didn't have feelings," he said, his voice coming from a much closer place than it had been only a moment before. He was standing right on the other side of the curtain, she could tell.

"But it's what you think, isn't it?"

"I may have a difficult time understanding feelings, or connecting with them, Charity. However, I never said you didn't have them. And I certainly didn't say it was because you were a con woman. You are the one who seems hellbent on identifying yourself as such as often as possible."

"So neither of us forget." She tugged her shirt up over her head, then made quick work of her pants, before taking the green dress off the hanger and undoing the zipper, stepping into the waterfall of rich silk.

"I am not likely to forget as it is the thing that brought us together. What a wonderful story for us to tell our child."

She pulled the dress up, holding it against her breasts, reaching behind her and trying to get a hold of the zipper tab.

She managed to get it partway up, but could not get the fabric to meet more than midway up her back. She arched, trying to contort herself so that she could get it up the rest of the way, rustling against the curtains as she did so.

"Let me help you," Rocco said, his voice softer, richer, darker than the crushed velvet that separated them.

"I'm fine."

"Don't be so damned stubborn," he said.

And then she felt his hands on the fabric of the gown, one braced on the base of the zipper, the other on the tab, as he quickly did it up. A lightning bolt of need shot through her as his knuckles brushed against her bare skin, only a fleeting touch, but it was enough. And not nearly enough all at the same time.

"There," he said, "it's much easier when you aren't stubborn, isn't it?"

She looked over her shoulder and was surprised by how close he was, his lips a whisper from hers now. "Easier, maybe. But it's not as much fun."

A smile curved his lips and she suddenly found herself being pushed deeper into the dressing room, his hold tight on her hip as he turned her to face him, pressing her back against the mirror. "You think this is fun?" He pressed his body against hers, and she could feel the hard length of his arousal against her stomach. "A little challenge?"

"What is life without a challenge?"

"Death," he said, leaning forward, scraping the sensitive skin of her neck with his teeth. "As long as we struggle we know we're still alive."

There was no doubt that she felt alive now. Her heart was thundering hard, her pulse racing, her core aching for something only he could give her.

"We can't do this here," she said, her voice strangled.

"I'm paying a lot for this room. I've paid less for hotel suites. All things considered, I can do whatever the hell I want here." He kissed her just beneath her jaw.

"This is a nice dress," she said.

"It would look nicer crumpled up on the floor."

"That won't help me choose," she said.

"I like your lips," he said, leaning in and kissing her hard, deep. When they parted, they were both breathing hard. "But I like them much better when they are wrapped around my dick."

Desire shot through her like an arrow, hitting its target straight on, the ache inside of her intensifying. But this was how things always went with him. He demanded; she acquiesced. He pushed and she gave way.

But not now. She would make him wait. She would make *him* beg.

"I have shopping to do," she said, leaning forward and taking his lower lip between her teeth, nipping him gently. "And you need to go sit out there and behave yourself. And tell me which dress you think looks best."

He growled, tightening his hold on her and pulling her firmly against his body. "Is that what I have to do?"

"Yes," she said, keeping her tone firm.

He released his hold on her and took a step back, his dark eyes glittering. "Have it your way." He turned and walked out of the dressing room, and for a moment she was afraid he had walked out altogether. Until she heard him settle in the chair.

She moved away from the mirror and turned to face it, so that she could get a look at the gown for the first time since she'd put it on. It was beautiful. Elegant. And not *her* at all.

Which was a strange thought to have, because she had only just been thinking that she wasn't certain who she was. But she was not this dress. That was all she knew.

She managed to unzip it on her own, and then stood in her underwear appraising the other garments that were available to her.

She reached out and touched one that looked like molten gold, the fabric shimmering as it moved beneath her fingertips. It was definitely flashy. Not something she would have gravitated toward under normal circumstances. Not unless she was trying to draw attention to herself for a con. But then, standing there, looking at all the dresses, she found she liked that one best. There was no reason for her to like it best. No brief that she was filling, except for her own.

And because there was no reason for her to like it other than that she simply did, she decided to try it next.

She removed it from the hanger and slipped it on. This one was strapless too, but the zipper was a little bit more cooperative. She removed her bra. The support built into the gown was all that was needed for her curves.

She looked up at her reflection in the mirror and her breath caught in her throat. Even without makeup, and without her hair done, she almost looked like a different person in the shimmering golden wonder. It lit up her complexion, catching the warmth in the brown tone of her skin and eyes.

She shifted and the light caught hold of the fabric, lighting the small space with a shower of sparkles. She tilted her head to the side and placed her hand on her hip, shifting her weight to her left leg. The fabric parted, revealing a high slit that ended well above her knee.

She liked this. And that hidden bit of daring meant that Rocco would probably like it, too.

She turned toward the curtains and walked out of the dressing room. Rocco was sitting in the chair, his posture casual, his manner disinterested. Until he lifted his gaze and saw her standing there.

Then his focus sharpened, his expression going as hard as stone.

"What do you think?" she asked. But she already knew what he thought. And it made her feel hot all over. Such an amazing thing, to be able to read the thoughts of another person so clearly. To be close enough to someone to be confident that she knew what he wanted.

And to know that what he wanted was her.

"You look very expensive," he said, his voice measured.

"There isn't a price tag on the dress. Which means it must be."

"That is not what I meant. The dress doesn't look expensive." He pushed against the arms of the chair and stood. "You look expensive. There are not many things I can't afford, Charity. But you look like you might be one of them."

"Is that a compliment, Rocco?"

He cupped her chin, tilted her face upward. His dark eyes were burning with the dark flame. "How could it be anything else?"

"Some women might not like the implication that they can be bought."

"That isn't what I was talking about. I like expensive things," he said, tracing her lower lip with his thumb. "Not because they represent status but…a certain amount of security. Stability." He moved his hand, pushing his fingers through her curls. "It shows that you are not…weak. Not helpless. I am a man who has spent his whole life collecting things. To show that I am no longer a boy in an empty house. A boy with no power. I am now a man who has all the power. All the wealth that one could possibly want. There is nothing I cannot have…but you. You are far beyond me. Beyond any man who will be at the gala tonight." He slid his palm over her cheek. "*Expensive* is perhaps… not the right word. *Priceless.* You look priceless."

Charity tried to breathe and found that she couldn't. Something shifted inside of her, an empty space filling. A part of her that had always felt reed thin, insubstantial and easily broken felt strengthened, wrapped up in his words as though they were spun gold, reinforcing her. Shielding her.

She had never felt valuable. From the first moment she could remember she had felt like a drain. Because her father had made it clear that having her cost him.

That she had to earn her keep. She didn't add to his life, she took away.

To have Rocco look at her and say that she had value… it was altering in a way she'd never imagined she needed.

"If I'm so costly…am I worth the trouble?" She knew she sounded insecure, desperate even… Right now she didn't care. She was testing this newfound strength inside of her. Seeing if it could grow even more. Seeing if he might build it up or knock it down. Seeing if she could withstand it either way.

"Everything worth having in life is trouble. It comes at high cost, at high risk and with much work. Easy things are for those too weak to mine life for all its richness. At least that's my take on it."

"I'll take this dress," she said, leaning in and pressing a kiss to his lips. "It had the exact effect I was looking for."

"It made me want you? Believe me when I say, I want you in or out of the dress, Charity. It doesn't matter what you're wearing."

"That isn't what I meant. It makes me feel special. It makes me feel like me. I like that. But you said some nice things, too."

A smile curved his lips. "As far as I'm concerned, that was damn poetry, woman."

"Noted. And appreciated." She closed her eyes and kissed him again, letting the feeling of closeness, the feeling of—if not camaraderie—not being at each other's throats, wash over her. "I guess we're done here then."

"Not quite." That smile of his turned wicked. "I was thinking perhaps you'd like a chance to choose some of your own lingerie, too."

CHAPTER EIGHT

THE GALA WAS a glittering affair. From the high-gloss marble floors to the pristine white pillars, to the chandeliers dripping with crystal hanging low from the ceilings. But nothing glittered brighter than the woman on his arm. Charity was the loveliest thing he had ever held in his possession. And he only realized as he walked into the crowded ballroom, filled with other people, how desperate he was to take her back home and lock the door. To put her up on a shelf in his home for safekeeping, so that no one and nothing could touch her.

He had recognized her value. And now that he had put her on display like this, so would everyone else. So would every other man here. And that made him feel… It made him feel as though something that was his was under threat of being stolen. And there was nothing on earth that filled him with greater anxiety than that. Even as they walked deeper into the room, it grabbed him by the throat like the jaws of a hungry wolf and shook him hard. Because it took him back. To helplessness and empty rooms. And the loss he could never quite recover from.

No, that won't happen. That's the whole point of gaining power.

The ballroom came back into focus, and it was only then that he'd realized darkness had been crowding around the edges of his vision. He tightened his hold on Charity's waist, moving his hands down around her hip, drawing her closer to him. She turned her head to look at him, her expression questioning.

She was so sensitive. Always looking for things in him that weren't there. Though, in this instance, he supposed they were. But, he was hardly going to confide in her. He was barely going to allow the thoughts to take hold in his own mind, let alone speak them out loud.

"Are you all right?" he asked, because turning it around her was infinitely preferable to examining himself.

"I'm fine," she said, her dark eyes moving to search the room. She was exquisitely made up tonight, compliments of the hair and makeup person he had brought in to help style her for the evening. She had been shocked, and slightly offended, but ultimately she had agreed, and the results were beyond anything he had imagined they might be.

Charity was always beautiful. Whether dressed in clothing sent by him to humiliate, or in her waitress uniform, with her face bare. But tonight, she was somewhere beyond beautiful. He had told her yesterday that she was expensive. Had added *priceless* in order to make her understand. But that had been closer to the truth than he'd realized. She *was* beyond price. Something a man could sell all of his possessions for and never hope to buy.

The makeup artist had used shades of gold and orange around her eyes, the color enhancing their deep brown. Her cheeks seemed to glow, her lips looked slick, the color of juicy citrus in the sun. Begging him to take a bite. Begging him to allow them to satisfy his thirst.

Her black hair had been tamed into sleek waves, left loose around her shoulders, one diamond pin keeping back a few curls, sparkling beneath the lights.

And that was to say nothing of the golden dress. It

looked like solid metal that had been melted down and poured over her curves, conforming to her skin, moving with her, the skirt billowing around her legs, the slit baring a tempting amount of tanned, toned thigh. All he wanted to do was grab her and pull her into a darkened corridor so he could take the gown off her and undo all the expert hair and makeup.

But, he supposed that ran counter to coming here in the first place.

Damn it all.

But he did need to stop her before they went out into the center of the room. Because he had one more thing for her. He almost didn't want to give it to her now, because she was perfect as she was, and he was afraid that adding to it might ruin the effect. Or worse, steal what was left of his control.

All the more reason he had to give it to her. To prove that he had not, by any stretch of the imagination, ceded any of his control to her.

"I have something for you," he said, bringing them both to a halt.

She looked up at him, surprise and something unreadable moving through her dark eyes. An answering emotion echoed in his stomach, and even while he felt it, he found he couldn't put a name to it. "You have something for me?" She looked down. "Don't I have enough from you? You've bought me all these clothes. You're paying for the medical care…"

"I'm not keeping a tally," he said, his voice harder than he would've liked. "At least, not beyond the million dollars your father stole from me."

"So, you are keeping a tally?"

"Only that one. This is not on it. Neither is the dress. And certainly the health care that you're receiving for the pregnancy, for our child, is not. Stop making me out to be more of a monster than I am."

She looked up at him again. "More of a monster? That seems to imply that you are a bit of one."

"You know as well as anyone that I am. A bit of one, anyway. And I have a gift for you." He reached into the interior pocket of his jacket and took out a slim, long velvet box. Charity's expression morphed from surprise to concern. "It is not a venomous serpent of any kind," he said.

"I didn't think it was."

"Then why are you looking at me like that?"

"No one has ever given me a gift before. And no, the lingerie you had sent to my house back in New York does not count."

"I would never have suggested it did." He frowned. "Surely someone has given you a gift before."

"Who would have?"

He had nothing to say to that. He had spent much of his childhood lonely. Without a mother. But he had had one for a while. And she had certainly given him presents. Yes, a great many of them had ended up being taken from him. But the act of her giving them to him... That could never be taken. Long after the things were gone, the gesture remained.

Charity had never even had the gesture. And so she was forced to receive it from him. A man who was not qualified in any way to be responsible for the emotional well-being of another person.

His stomach twisted, and he opened the box quickly. "It's just a necklace," he said. He wanted to minimize the gesture now, so she would stop looking at him that way. Expectantly. As though she expected him to know what to do now. As though she expected him to know what to say, as though she expected him to have some sort of remedy for the things that hurt her.

"It's beautiful," she said, her voice a whisper, her eyes soft.

He wanted to tell her to stop doing that. And yet, at the same time he wanted her to look at him like that forever.

None of it made any sense. And he didn't have the time to sort through it now, in a crowded ballroom.

"You should wear it," he said, taking it out of the box and undoing the clasp.

"Okay. If you think it goes with my dress," she said, wringing her hands in front of her as though she were nervous.

"I chose it to go with the dress," he said. "Of course it goes with the dress."

He turned to face her, holding the necklace out and placing it gently around her neck. He kept his eyes locked with hers as he worked on the clasp until he was certain it was secured.

He had chosen a heavy, teardrop-shaped emerald, one he had known would settle perfectly between her breasts once the dress was removed. He had lied about it being chosen to go with the dress. He had chosen it to go with her body. With her skin.

He had chosen it because of how she would look later, wearing only that.

But he had a feeling if he said that, the look of wonder and gratitude would slide right off her beautiful face, and he didn't want to see that happen. If he mentioned it, he would wait until it was dark. Until he couldn't see. Or, he would wait until he had her mindless with pleasure.

He reached out and slipped his fingers beneath the gem, testing its weight in his palm, before placing it gently back against her skin.

"Perfect," he said, taking a step back.

She was. Indescribably so. Of course, now he had ensured that he would not be able to think of anything else but her, bare and wearing only that necklace. But then, the odds were high that all he would have been thinking about was her naked whether or not he had given her the necklace.

"Thank you," she said. She was so sincere. And he wasn't sure what to do with that. Sincerity usually skimmed right over his hardened veneer of cynicism, but hers had managed to find cracks he had not realized were there. He didn't like it. But his liking it didn't seem to be a factor.

"You're welcome," he said, knowing he sounded less than gracious. "Shall we?" He extended his arm, looking away from her and at a crowd of people at the center of the room.

He felt delicate fingers curled around his forearm, and he swallowed hard, using every bit of his strength to keep from looking at her. He led them both down the stairs and into the center of the room. And it didn't take long for the devils in suits to notice that he had dropped a particularly beautiful angel in their midst.

But she was not for them. None of the assholes in here were worthy of her. Hell, he wasn't worthy of her. But if anyone was going to defile her sweetness it was going to be him. Because she belonged to him.

He tightened his hold on her as they moved deeper into the crowd.

Leon Carides, a businessman from Greece who Rocco had had vague dealings with in the past, locked his eyes onto Charity, then looked back at Rocco, a slow smile spreading over his lips as he separated himself from the group he was talking to and made his way toward them.

"Amari," he said, his focus now firmly back on Charity, "nice to see you here. And you've brought a guest. You normally come to these events alone."

"Not tonight," Rocco said.

"Clearly. Leon Carides."

"Charity Wyatt," she returned, holding out her hand as she had done to the woman in the boutique yesterday. Really, the only time he had ever seen her betray any signs of weakness was with him. And he was under no illusion that initially she had been using it to try and manipulate him. But later, when she had come to tell him about the pregnancy, when he had gone to see her in the doctor's office, she had shown him her vulnerability. And he was only just now realizing how rare that was.

"Pleasure," Leon said, holding on to Charity's hand much longer than Rocco would have liked. In fact, he was contemplating separating the other man's hand from his wrist when he finally released his hold on her.

"Did you have business you wanted to discuss, Carides?"

"Not particularly," the other man said, his eyes still fixed on Charity. "Though, I must say, I'm surprised that you brought a date. You seem to prefer stealing mine at the end of the night to bringing your own."

For some reason Rocco bristled at the mention of his past behavior. He didn't want it brought out in the open in front of Charity. Which was stupid. Especially since she knew exactly what manner of man he was, both because of his own words and because of the deeds he had committed against her.

Still, he didn't appreciate Leon trotting it out for her examination.

"If you think you're going to return the favor, Carides, think again."

"That would be up to your guest, don't you suppose?" Leon asked, his eyes glittering as he appraised Charity.

"His guest who is standing right here," Charity said, her tone crisp. "And thank you for the offer, if it was indeed an offer. I'm flattered."

"Oh, it was," said Leon. "Do you have an answer for me?"

"No," Rocco said. "Her answer is no."

He felt Charity stiffen beneath his touch. But he didn't really care if she was angry with him. All that really mattered was that Leon understood that Charity belonged to him and would be going home with no one else.

"I can speak for myself," she said.

"You didn't speak fast enough," he said, his voice hard.

"Rocco…"

"Trouble in paradise—a shame," Leon said. "If you have a different answer than your minder here," he said, directing the words at Charity, "do come and look for me before you leave." He turned and walked away, leaving Rocco standing there vibrating with rage.

"I don't need you to answer for me," Charity said, her voice low.

"I gave you a gift, I can do whatever I like," he said, knowing he was being unreasonable and not caring at all.

"I will give it back if that's how you see things. It was my understanding that gifts came without strings attached."

"How would you know, as this is the first one you have ever received?"

For a moment, he saw hurt, deep and raw flash through her dark eyes before she put her mask back on, leaving her face smooth, unreadable. "I regret telling you that," she said.

He wanted to tell her not to regret it. He wanted to apologize. But he didn't know what that would accomplish. Only a few moments ago she had looked at him as though she wanted something from him, something emotional and deep. And just now he had proven he was not the man to give her that. It was for the best.

Decadence he could give her. Pleasure he could give her. Clothing, jewelry, he could give her. As for the rest? He didn't even know what the rest was.

"I wish I could give you something more substantial than that regret," he said, and in this instance he was being truthful. "Sadly, I feel if you're looking for anything more than physical satisfaction with me, regret is all you will find."

"I'll keep that in mind. I wonder if it's the same for Leon. Something to consider, as I seem to have an open invitation."

Rocco slid his hand up her spine, taking hold of the back of her neck. "Tell me, *cara*, do you want the father of your child arrested and sent to prison for murder?"

Her eyes flared wide. "No."

"Then do not tempt me to kill Leon Carides." Charity opened her mouth to speak, but he decided he was done talking. "Shall we dance?"

"That is…not what I expected you to say next."

"Does it matter what you expected? Come and dance with me. It is not a request. Or have you forgotten that I still hold the power in this arrangement?" He was being an asshole, and he knew it. But he couldn't seem to moderate his own behavior at the moment, and that was disconcerting.

"How could I forget, as you're so good at reminding me?"

She was angry with him, but she allowed him to lead her to the dance floor. Allowed him to pull her close, so that her breasts were pressed against his chest. She even wrapped her arms around his neck, feigning compliance. But he knew that it wasn't real. Knew that she was only pretending to be brought to heel. Probably so she could get close enough to him to strangle him.

He slid his hand down the curve of her lower back, to her ass, pushing her more tightly to him, allowing her to feel the arousal that was coursing through his body in spite of his anger. He was hard for her. But then, he was always hard for her.

She drew her head back, anger glittering in her eyes, even while her pupils expanded, her desire for him evident, as evident as her anger. Fine. He didn't care if she liked him. He only needed her to want him.

"You don't seem to care," he said, moving them both in time with the music.

"Of course I care. A prisoner can never forget she's in jail."

The light of challenge in her eyes spurred him on. "But you are not in jail, my dear, or have you forgotten? You could be. But you are not."

She lifted her chin, her expression haughty. "Am I supposed to get on my knees and thank you?"

"It all depends on what you intend to do while you're down there."

"Ensure that you're incapable of fathering any more children?"

"Oh, we both know you won't do that. That part of my body is far too valuable to you. As you have proven over the past week. Repeatedly." He leaned in and pressed a kiss to her lips. "You might not like me, Charity. But you can't resist me." He was driven to push her now, to strike out at her because the whole experience with Leon had burned him deep down in his chest and since he had no idea how to heal that pain, he had decided to keep on burning everything until he went numb.

"Keep talking. A few more well-placed phrases and I bet I'll be able to resist you permanently."

"We both know that isn't true. If you couldn't resist me that day at The Mark, you won't be able to resist me now." He said it as if it was a certainty, but really, it was a question. And he hated himself for feeling the need to ask it.

But he needed to know that he had her. That no matter what, she wouldn't turn away from him. That he was as irresistible to her as she was to him.

"You seem determined to push me until I can."

"Does it seem that way? That is not my intent." Or perhaps it was. Something, anything to get a handle on his control.

Why did this woman test it? Shatter it?

"Then maybe you could try being nice for a while," she said.

"I don't know how to be nice," he said. "I've never had to be."

"You can start by not making death threats to men we meet at parties. And then you can finish by not behaving as though you have the right to control my actions."

"I don't think you understand, *cara.* You are mine." He raised his hand and cupped her cheek. "And when someone tries to steal what is mine I do not respond kindly. Leon was treading on dangerous ground."

"But I'm not an object, Rocco. He isn't going to just pick me up and make off with me."

"He might. He is a wealthy man. He would have a lot to offer you."

"I thought I was priceless, Rocco. Why are you acting as though I can be bought?"

"You seemed interested," he bit out.

"I'm not. Not in a man who won't hold my hair when I throw up the morning after he's spent the night holding me in his arms. And I'm insulted that you would think I might be tempted to go with him."

He looked past her. "Why would I ever think differently? I don't know you."

"That's insulting," she said, her voice soft. Wounded. It touched him somewhere down deep, and he realized he was not yet numb. No matter how much he wished he were. "You know me better than anyone."

Her words hit him with the force of a slap. "Do I?"

"How can you ask that? You're the only man I've ever been with. You know that."

"In my experience sex has nothing to do with how well you know someone."

"Maybe not to you. But it does to me. I already told you why I was never with another man. I told you...I feel like you've been standing by watching as I discover who I am. How could you not know me?" Her eyes were luminous, filled with emotion.

Her words grabbed ahold of something inside of him and twisted hard. "I want to show you something."

The open emotion transformed into a near-comical scowl. "If it's your penis I'm going to go ahead and say no thank you."

He laughed, somewhat reluctantly. He wasn't sure how he could be so angry, aroused and amused all at once. He was not sure how he had wound up here, feeling like this, with a woman he had intended to hate. "Well, I will probably offer to show you that after. But that is not what I meant." He didn't know why he was making this offer, except perhaps as some kind of desperate last attempt to undo the damage he had done over the past half hour. To try and recapture the look on her face when he had given her the necklace. The look he had never deserved, the look he had proved he didn't deserve only moments afterward.

Truly, feelings made no sense. And he was getting tired of having them.

"Okay, you can show me something," she said, her expression softening. "Anything."

Her words flooded his chest with a burst of warmth. "We'll just finish this song then."

And for the rest of the dance, he held her close. And they didn't say anything. And for a few moments at least, he thought she might not just want him, but she might like him, too.

Charity wasn't sure what had transpired between her and Rocco at the gala tonight. Yes, they had fought, but in some ways she felt closer to him now than she had before they had left the house. He had given her a gift. He had insulted her. He had made her feel things. Had made her angry, had made her happy, had made her sad. Like a miniature relationship ecosystem all contained in the ballroom of a hotel.

And now they were back at the villa. And she wasn't sure what was going to happen next. There had been something strange in his tone when he'd told her he had something to show her. Strange enough that she'd been an idiot and tried to defuse the tension with humor.

Because she was still uncomfortable when things got close to the bone. When things got real, authentic. She was so accustomed to slipping on different masks, using them to shield her from anything unpleasant, that she seemed to default to it easily.

"What is it you want to show me?" she asked, pausing in the vast entryway.

"My things," he said, the bland note in his voice betraying more than outward emotion. Because he was like her. He put a mask on most especially when he was feeling deeply. And that was what he had done the moment they had walked inside.

This was important to him.

She frowned. "What things?"

"All of them. Of course, you've been living in my home for the past week. So you have seen some. But...just come with me."

He walked on ahead of her, down a hallway she had never gone down before. Because she had had no reason to. She wrapped her arms around her waist to try and keep herself warm. Because for some reason she felt an unaccountable chill.

Rocco stopped in front of a set of double doors. He turned to face her, a muscle ticking in his jaw. There was a keypad by the door and he entered in a series of numbers quickly, and she heard a lock release.

"Internal security?"

"Yes," he said. "I told you, no one steals from me."

Of course, that was very like her father. To rip off a man who clearly had more than just your average issue with being stolen from. But on the heels of that thought came another one. One that ripped through her like a ravenous beast. There was a reason for this.

She flashed back to what he had told her about when his mother died. When they had taken him from his home, when they had taken all of his things... She looked up at him, a wave of horror washing over her. He looked away from her and pulled the doors open.

She moved behind him, wrapping her arms around his waist and resting her head between his shoulder blades. She was shaking, and she hadn't even seen what he was about to show her. "You don't have to," she said, her heart thundering fast now.

She wasn't sure if she was trying to spare him, or her.

Because when she saw, once all of the pieces that she had been collecting of him were complete, once she was able to fit them all together, the vague yearning that was in her chest would be complete, too. Would turn into something else. Something she didn't want to think about.

"I want to show you," he said, his voice rough.

He released his hold on the door and stepped out of her embrace, walking into the room.

There was framed art on the wall, figurines in glass cases, vases. Coin collections, swords mounted onto the wall. Basically anything that could be considered collectible was here, except for cars. Though, she knew he had his share of those in his garage. She wasn't sure what she had expected, but it wasn't this.

"I collect things," he said, "expensive things. Any expensive thing really. I told you already, when my mother died I lost everything. I spent most of my life with nothing that belonged to me. My bedrooms were shared with other children. And more than that, they were temporary. I had no family. I had nothing. I felt helpless. Like there was nothing keeping me from drifting out to sea. As I became more successful, I realized that I could fix that. I bought myself a house. Now I own four houses. And I have my own bedroom in all of them. And nobody sleeps in them but me."

Charity realized then that she had never spent time in his room. Always when they slept together it was in her room. Her stomach twisted. And he continued.

"And I began to collect things. Things to replace what I lost. To make me feel like I was here." His dark eyes met hers. "I protect what belongs to me."

She kept thinking of what he had said at the gala. That she was his. That she belonged to him. It had seemed offensive, dismissive and minimizing. But she could see now that to him it meant something much deeper than it would to anyone else.

These things, these things that belonged to him, he protected above everything else. He prized them.

She turned in a circle, trying to take in the vast collection. "It's amazing," she said.

"Is it?" he asked. "I confess, I don't enjoy what I have in here very often. Though, I frequently check to make sure it's all still here."

His words made her feel as if someone had reached into her chest, grabbed her heart and squeezed it tight. She could barely breathe. She looked at the far corner of the room and saw a pedestal, with a glass case over the top. But she couldn't tell what was underneath it.

She took a step forward, her breath catching when she recognized what was beneath the glass case. Army men. Little green plastic army men that had no value. At least not monetary value.

"Rocco…"

He looked away, color staining his cheeks. "They were my favorite. They were the things I missed the most. Except for my mother. But…they were what I missed the most that I could replace." He looked back at her, his dark eyes hollow. "So, now you see."

"Yes," she said.

And she was certain they weren't just talking about the collection.

"Rocco…"

He closed the distance between them, his expression fierce, pulling her hard up against his body, cupping her cheek with his large warm hand. "Don't."

"Don't what?"

"Whatever you were going to do. Kiss me instead."

So she did. She rose up on her tiptoes and kissed him with everything she had in her. He sifted his fingers through her hair, holding her tightly to him as he kissed her deep, hard. He was shaking, and she was sure that she was, too. He moved his hand down to cup her chin briefly, then trace the line of her throat with his fingertips, before they came to rest on the jewel at the center of her necklace.

"Perfect," he said, his tone intense. "And mine." And she realized, through the haze of her arousal, that he didn't mean the necklace. "If only I could keep you here as securely as I do everything else I possess."

Her heart fluttered in her chest, fear joining the desire that was roaring through her. She had a feeling he was sincere. That he would lock her in a glass case if he could, and yet, she didn't want to run from him. Because that would mean being without him. And she didn't want that, either.

She had been right about understanding him. Had been right about what it would make her feel. Or rather, understanding him had given her a name for her feelings.

She was afraid that she loved him. And worse than that, she wanted him to love her back.

She was a stupid girl. She had wanted her father to love her, had wanted the love of her mother, a mother who had never even been there. Wanted too the love of a grandmother who had only ever taken her in sporadically so that she wouldn't end up sleeping alone on the streets.

For so much of her life, she had craved the love of people who wouldn't give it to her. And now, she was adding one more to the list.

Rocco.

The father of her child. Her lover. The only man who knew her at all.

Her heart suddenly felt too big for her chest, her eyes

stinging with tears she refused to shed. Her head ached, her body ached.

Maybe none of them love you back because you don't deserve to be loved back.

She gritted her teeth and closed her eyes against the insidious voice that was shouting loudly inside of her. Finally putting into words what she had always believed in her heart to be true.

Surely if she were lovable, someone would've loved her by now.

She was a thief. She was guilty. She had stolen from this man who prized his possessions above all else. This man who had lost quite enough.

He could never possibly feel the same for her as she did for him, not knowing the extent of what she was.

No. She wouldn't think of that now.

Anyway, this moment wasn't all about her. This was about him. He had given her so much of himself in this moment. And she had to honor that gift.

"I'm sorry," she said, words pouring out of her now. "I'm sorry I stole from you. I had no right to take anything from you. And I have no excuse. I can't hide behind my father. I can't hide behind my upbringing. Because I knew it was wrong, and I did it anyway. I'm sorry," she said, repeating the apology over and over again.

She didn't care if he could use this against her. Didn't care if she was giving him evidence to put her in jail forever. All that mattered now was that she make it right. In the only way she could. She couldn't return the money, but she could admit what she'd done. Could confess it all to him, lay herself bare, as he had just done for her.

"I know it was wrong," she said, more for her now than for him. "And I'm not going to do it again. I've changed.

I really have." She had to believe it. She needed to say it, because she needed it to be true.

"I know you stole the money," he said, his dark eyes meeting hers. "It doesn't matter."

"Yes it does," she said.

He cut her words off with a fierce kiss, still holding the gem on her necklace. "No," he said, resting his forehead against hers, "you are not a con woman. You have done dishonest things. I believe that you have conned people. I believe you conned me. But those cons…they are just things you've done. They are not *you*."

She swallowed hard, her throat so tight she could barely breathe. "I don't deserve that."

"Life is nothing but a series of things we don't deserve. Both good and bad. I say we take the good when it comes, because God knows the bad is never far behind."

"I don't…"

"Just accept it. Accept this," he said, kissing her again.

She squeezed her eyes shut, kissing him back, drowning in him, in this. In the atonement that he offered. He was right, after all. Nothing of life was fair. She had accepted that in terms of the bad, and this was good. So she should take it. While it was here. Touch some of the brightness before it all slipped back into shadow.

Rocco gripped his tie and loosened it, and she helped him pull it through his collar, casting it down onto the floor. Her fingers went to the buttons of his shirt, clumsily undoing two of them, her hands shaking.

She didn't know what the future held, but she knew she wanted this. She knew that she loved him. And she knew that she wanted this moment. Beyond that, she didn't care.

He lowered them to the rug that covered the marble floor, not breaking their kisses as he did so. He settled over her, her skirt falling back, the split parting, revealing her leg. Rocco placed his hand on her thigh, the warmth of his touch burning through her skin, through her entire body.

"I have a fantasy," he said, "of seeing you wearing nothing but this necklace."

His words heated her body further, filled that empty place inside of her that was so hungry for someone to care. For someone to want her. She was his fantasy.

You're mine.

And she knew now what that meant to him. Knew now that it was not meant to lessen the connection between them, because she had seen for herself just what a claim of ownership meant to him.

"It's an easy fantasy to see realized," she said, kissing him just below the line of his square jaw.

He reached behind her and tugged on the zipper of her dress, pulling the garment that would have cost a couple months of her waitressing wages down and discarding it in a molten gold ball on the floor. She wasn't wearing a bra, nothing other than a black thong that was little more than a sheer whisper of lace, framing her body more than it concealed it. He curled his fingers over the waistband of her panties, rough skin brushing the most sensitive part of her as he dragged them down her legs.

"Yes," he said, his breath hissing through his teeth, dark eyes intent on her body. "This is exactly what I wanted." He reached up and touched the necklace, weighing it in his hands. "This is exactly how I thought it would look." He let it fall between her breasts, the jewel warm from his touch. "I like having you here, with my collection. You are mine, Charity."

She lifted her hand and pressed it to his chest, over his shirt, and she could feel his heart raging beneath her palm. "Mine," she said, the word even more feral on her lips than it had been on his. "If you think you can take possession of me, then I will damn well take it of you."

"You have it," he said. "Though, I'm not sure why you would want it."

"Is that a gift?"

"Yes." He kissed her neck, the curve of her breast. "It is."

"I'm up to two then."

He straightened, undoing the rest of the buttons on his shirt and discarding it. Then he put his hands on his belt, working it free as he took his shoes and socks off, making quick work of his pants and underwear, so soon he was as bare as she was. "All of this is yours, if you want." She looked at him, his broad shoulders, his hard, well-defined muscles. His dark, intense eyes. "Say you want me," he said, a note of desperation in his tone.

"You know I do," she said.

"I need you to say it. Because the first time you felt like you had to strip for me. Now I want you here, naked, because you want to be."

"I do. I want you."

It was all the permission he needed. He groaned and kissed her, covering her body with his, easing her thighs apart as he settled between them. He moved his hand to palm her breast, squeezing her nipple between his thumb and forefinger. A sharp shock of pleasure rocked her, curling itself around the emotion that was expanding in her chest, until they were inextricably linked. She would never be able to separate the two again. Pleasure like this would always belong to Rocco, would always be part of the love that she felt for him. The love that she craved from him.

He bent his head, sliding his tongue around one tight bud, then drawing it deeply into his mouth. "Mine," he said. Then he kissed her lower, beneath her rib cage, beneath her belly button, moving lower still until his lips were hovering over the most sensitive part of her. "Mine," he said again, the word nearly a growl.

He lowered his head, tasting her deep, teasing the sensitive bundle of nerves at the apex of her thighs before delving deeper still, penetrating her damp core with his tongue. She gasped, arching into him, moving in time with him.

He lifted his head, turned and bit her inner thigh, the sharp jolt of pain rocking her, pushing her closer to climax.

"Mine," he said. "All of you. All for me."

He moved back to her mouth, kissing her deeply, the evidence of her own arousal there on his lips.

He thrust deep inside her and she gasped, his possession pushing her over the edge, pleasure roaring through her as she lost herself in this, in him.

In being his.

He kept his eyes locked with hers as he chased his own release, clenching his jaw tight, the fingers of one hand buried deeply in her hair, the other hand holding firmly to her hip.

"Mine, Charity, all mine," he said, the words ending on a harsh groan as he gave himself up to his own pleasure. He closed his eyes, his body shuddering out its climax, his shaft pulsing deep inside of her as he gave up his control utterly, completely.

He had taken possession of her, but he had given her some of himself.

He had given her a gift.

He was the only one who ever had.

She wrapped her arms around his neck and held him close. The carpet was starting to feel scratchy beneath her back, possibly because her skin was raw from the intensity of their lovemaking. And he was starting to get heavy, his skin hot against hers, slick with sweat. But she didn't want him to move. She wanted to freeze this moment forever.

It was the happiest moment of her entire life. She realized that with the harsh, sudden force of a blow.

In this moment her entire future stretched out before her, and in it, she wasn't alone. Because right now, with Rocco as close to her as she could possibly be to another human being, it was impossible to imagine being alone. Right now she had him and their baby. She had security. She had passion.

She had more right now—or at least the promise of more—than ever before. And she was treasuring this moment of possibility more than she could have ever fathomed treasuring anything.

After a long while he shifted position, pulling her against him, wrapping his arm around her waist, his chin resting on her shoulder. She could have stayed like that forever. Barring that, she would take it for the next few hours.

She didn't sleep. She simply lay there in Rocco's arms, trying to will the sun to stay sunken into the sea. Because as long as the darkness was drawn over them like a blanket, it felt as if time was standing still.

And when the sky started to turn a lighter shade of gray, she closed her eyes, so she could pretend again.

But inevitably, she knew the time would pass. She knew this moment would pass. And all of the incredible possibilities would dissolve, as future became the present.

But not now. Right now, she was in Rocco's arms.

And that was all she would think about.

CHAPTER NINE

CHARITY'S PHONE RANG at about three in the morning. Rocco opened his eyes and looked through the dark, his eyes focusing on the ceiling. But he didn't move. Beside him, she groaned and stirred, and he felt the mattress depressing as she sat up.

"Hello?" Her voice was gruff, sleepy, and he found it unaccountably sexy. "What do you want? Why are you calling me?" Abruptly, her voice sharpened. He felt her get out of bed, and he remained motionless.

"I could be in jail for all you know," she said, her tone a fierce whisper now. "Not that you bothered to check."

Her father. It had to be her father. He didn't move. He wanted her to stay in the room, to keep talking. Mostly, he wanted to take the phone out of her hand and yell at the man on the other end.

And it wasn't so he could get his money back.

For some reason, in this moment, Rocco was angry because that man had left his own daughter to take the fall for his actions.

And you made sure it was quite a fall.

His stomach twisted, guilt turning over inside of him.

"You would have seen it on the news? That's nice."

The door to the bedroom opened, and Charity's voice became fainter.

He rolled sideways, swinging his legs over the edge of the mattress and standing. Then he made his way to the door, keeping his footsteps silent. She had left it open a crack, and he took full advantage of that, lingering in the shadow as he did the best he could to catch the rest of her conversation, filtering in from the hallway.

"You have to return the money," she was saying now.

His breath caught in his chest, settling there like a rock. If her father returned the money, much of his leverage would be gone.

Certainly, legally he would still have a claim, but the entire goal was to see the return of his property. At least, in the beginning it had been. And Charity knew that.

The simple fact was, he would not have her thrown in jail. Not now. He would protect her, no matter what. But, if she *knew* that, she might not stay. And that was unacceptable.

He needed his leverage.

"He knows. He knows who I am." There was a pause. "I'm with him now." Another pause. "None of your damn business what I'm doing with him."

He assumed her father was speaking again. "Yes, as a matter of fact I am sleeping with him. Again, not that it's your business." She paced a few steps. "His whore? That's rich coming from you. You're a thief. And you're really trying to take the moral high ground? Return the money. Because if there's one thing I can't do, it's protect you from him. He'll do what he wants. I don't have any control over it."

She must have hung up, because a moment later she put her hand down to her side and he heard her whisper a short, sharp curse.

Rocco turned away from the door and got back into bed, waiting for her to return.

"Who was that?" he asked, waiting to see what she would say.

"No one," she said, getting into bed beside him.

Disappointment gripped his throat, and he wasn't sure why.

Maybe he was disappointed because, as far as he could tell, there had been no reason for her to keep the phone call a secret. Except that she didn't trust him.

"Wrong number?" he asked.

"Yes," she said, her voice muted. "No," she said abruptly, rolling over to her side. "It was my father. I'm sorry, lying to you seemed easier."

A rush of relief flooded him. "I know, I was eavesdropping. In the spirit of honesty," he said, "I figured I should confess, too."

"Oh. You were going to let me get away with lying?"

"Yes."

"He didn't tell me anything. He wanted to see if you had found out. And I told him you had. He says he doesn't have the money anymore. And, as I'm sure you could tell from my tone, he isn't sorry at all that he left me to fend for myself. He had some choice names for me, actually."

"You are not my whore," he said, anger like a ball of molten steel in his chest. "And I am sorry that I ever used the word in connection with you. I am sorry I called you that. I was angry, and I was trying to hurt you. And I knew that those words would be hurtful. Especially after what I had done." He paused. "I know what it is to be at a disadvantage in life. The fact that I ever put you in that position, where you felt you had to trade your body for your freedom… It was unconscionable. Though I confess freely that I'm a man who has been out of touch with his conscience for a great many years. But I never thought I would become one of those men who took advantage of women in quite this way."

"Thank you," she said, burying her face in his shoulder. "Thank you."

He was sorry. And he regretted the way he had started things between them, and yet he couldn't regret the place they were in now. And he also couldn't let her go. An impossible situation.

"I'm not sure I deserve to be thanked."

"Well, you were wrong. And you were a...a...an absolute beast. And sometimes you still are. But I was hardly an angel. I stole from you. And I lied to you. And I played as innocent as I could in order to make you feel sorry for me. And then, when we went to your hotel room...I forgot everything. I know it started out...like it did. But once we were there...once you kissed me...I forgot everything but wanting you. You didn't force me. You know you didn't."

"I never get tired of hearing that." He laughed, a hollow, humorless sound. "So, the fact that you have to tell me that says an awful lot about my character."

"We went over this already. Neither of us had the best of characters when we first met."

"I disagree," he said. "You're a very strong woman. You have made some bad decisions, but I think your character was always strong. To survive the childhood you did..."

"I admit it wasn't all roses and daffodils. But plenty of people go through hard times and never end up turning to a life of crime."

"And plenty of people have money stolen from them without blackmailing the thief into bed."

"I can't get your money back," she said, her voice wound tight with regret. "I don't even know where he is."

"Then you must stay with me. Marry me." He had not intended to propose, but the words came out of their own accord, and the moment they did, he realized how very badly he wanted her to say yes. And so, he did what he did best; he took away her choice. "You must. It is the only way you can make restitution for what you took from me."

"Is this a proposal, or more blackmail? It's very hard to tell with you."

"It's a little of both."

"It didn't sound like it was a question."

He wrapped his arms around her and pulled her close. "It wasn't."

"What's the benefit of marriage?"

"I told you, Charity. You are mine now." He closed his eyes, gritting his teeth against the intense wave of feelings that were coursing through him. He wasn't used to this. To wanting quite so fiercely. Not anymore. He had got himself to a position in life where he didn't want anymore. He had. He possessed. He was unaccustomed to feeling as though he was lacking something, but he did now. For some strange reason, he felt as if he was back at square one, scrabbling alone in a dark empty room desperately seeking purchase.

And it made no sense, because he was holding Charity in his arms right now. And yet he could feel something was missing.

It should be simple. As easy as buying a beautiful painting, but it wasn't. Because even with her here and now, physically, he felt that it wasn't complete. It should all fit together. It should all make sense, and yet it didn't.

"Marriage seems like a good way of making it permanent," he said finally.

Making her his wife. That would solve it. Turning the lock, ensuring she couldn't simply leave. More insurance.

"Okay," she said.

"Is that your answer?"

"It wasn't a question. You already said that."

"No," he said, confirming it yet again. "It wasn't." And

yet, he couldn't shake the feeling that a yes from her lips would have been much sweeter than forced compliance.

But if he asked the question, he had to accept the fact that her answer could be no.

He was not prepared to take that risk.

"When do you want to get married then?" she asked.

"Before the baby is born," he said.

The sooner they made it official the better. It might do something to ease the panic that was rioting through him.

"I suppose I'll need a dress."

Some of the pressure in his chest eased. "Well, as it happens I know where you can get one of those."

He closed his eyes again, relishing the warm weight of Charity's hand on his chest.

Soon she would have a ring to go with her necklace. And the entire world would know that she belonged to him.

Charity was having her fitting for her wedding gown, and Rocco was not allowed to attend. Which meant he was planning on going anyway. Currently, he had been banished from her room until the seamstress was finished with the fitting.

It would be a small wedding. They had already decided. It wasn't as though Rocco had any friends to invite. Though, there were business associates who would be terribly offended if they weren't allowed to attend.

The media would, whether they wanted them to or not, make a big song and dance about the legendary playboy Rocco Amari settling down and committing for life, so they would have to at least make a show of a genuine wedding anyway. Inevitably, the truth about the baby would come out, too. Particularly since Charity was beginning to show, and three weeks from now when the ceremony was actually held he imagined the evidence of her pregnancy would be even more significant.

He could no longer wait to see her. And he was a man who never did what he didn't want to do. He turned and headed back toward her bedroom, flinging the doors open wide without knocking.

Charity looked up, her dark eyes wide with shock, and so did the woman who was kneeling at the hem of Charity's dress, tugging pins out of the fabric.

Charity's dark curls were loose and wild, a couple of wildflowers tucked into her glossy mane, bright pink lipstick highlighting her beautiful mouth. The dress was simple, a light flowing fabric that skimmed the increasingly full curves of her body. The dress was tight just beneath her breasts, then looser around her stomach, beautifully displaying the changes that had taken place in her body over the past weeks.

There was something highly sensual about it, and it sent an elemental heat firing through his blood.

His woman, in a wedding gown, pregnant with his child.

All of it increased the intensity of the word that was constantly echoing inside of him, whenever he looked at her. *Mine.*

"Beautiful," he said, because it was all he could say.

"You weren't supposed to come in," she said, clearly annoyed with him.

"We do all kinds of things out of order. Why would we be expected to observe tradition in this?" he asked, moving deeper into the room.

"Maybe because I asked you not to?" She arched a brow, her tone full of censure.

"I do not take direction well, Charity, a fact you should know by now. Are you finished?" He directed the question to the seamstress.

"Yes, but I will need to take the dress so that I can make the alterations."

"I will help her undress. You are dismissed," he said.

The woman nodded and stood, making her way out of the room quickly.

"Well, you are in an extra autocratic mood today."

He shrugged a shoulder. "Am I different than usual?"

"I guess not."

"I did not want her in here while I gave you this. Neither did I want to wait to give it to you." He reached into his jacket pocket and pulled out a ring box. "Speaking of things we have done out of order." He opened it and revealed the ring inside. An emerald that did, indeed, match her necklace.

Charity just stood there staring at him, blinking slowly. "Am I supposed to just take it?"

"Do you want me to put it on you?" He found, that as soon as he said the words, he wanted very much to take her hand in his and slip the ring onto her finger himself.

"It isn't necessary," she said, reaching out and taking the ring between her thumb and forefinger. He gritted his teeth against the disappointment that assaulted him. She slipped it onto her fourth finger, and held it out in front of her. "It's beautiful," she said. "You have very good taste in jewelry."

"Yes, well, I am a connoisseur of nice things. That was a compliment by the way."

She arched her dark brows. "Was it?"

"You do not seem happy with me," he said.

"Do I not? I am. I'm fine."

"Do not lie to me. I'm tired of dishonesty between us."

She let out an exasperated breath. "All right, I'm a little bit dazed. This is all happening very quickly."

"It has to happen quickly. You said you wanted to get married before the baby was born."

"I never actually said I wanted to get married," she said, her words hitting him with the force of a slap.

"And I do not recall asking," he said, his words hard.

"No, you didn't."

He turned away from her and began to pace the length of the room. "But you want this."

"Does it matter?"

He whirled back around. "What are your other options? To go back to your hovel in Brooklyn? To go to prison?"

"I don't have other options," she said, her tone grave.

For some reason a piece of memory hit him. Strangers picking him up, carrying him out of his house.

"Everything will be fine," he said, almost in time with the strangers in his head.

Everything will be okay.

But nothing was ever okay again.

"I'm sure it will be," she said, her dark eyes blank.

"What is wrong with you? You were fine last time we spoke about this. You were fine this morning."

"It all feels very real now."

"So the past few weeks of living with me, carrying my child, sharing a bed, did not feel real?"

"You know what I mean. This feels permanent." She blinked more rapidly now, her brown eyes getting glossy. "In some ways I can't really believe the past four months have happened at all. And I can't believe... Never mind."

"No. Tell me."

"Or what? You'll have me thrown in prison?"

"If I were you it would be a very real concern."

"But it isn't a concern. Because I'm doing what you ask."

Her words landed in that hollow place inside of him,

that empty void that he seemed to be becoming more and more aware of. A void that had been hiding for years, one that he had hidden beneath his status, his collections, his possessions. Things that he could see now had done nothing to actually fill that void.

"See that you continue to do so." He turned away from her, and she reached out and put her hand on his forearm, her fingers curling into the sleeve of his shirt. "What?" he asked.

"Do you want to marry me?" He turned to look at her, and was hit full on with the force of the emotion in her dark eyes. "I mean, do you want to be with me? Or is this just you doing what you can to keep control?"

"Of course I want control."

"Are you going to be faithful to me?"

He hadn't specifically thought about it, not since their initial conversation when he had said he would continue to behave as he had always done. But, the truth was he had no desire to be with anyone else.

"Yes, and you will be faithful to me," he said.

"Another edict?"

"It damn well is," he said through gritted teeth.

"You didn't answer my first question, though. Do you *want* me?"

He lifted his hand and cupped her cheek, tracing her lower lip with his thumb. It was so soft. *She* was so soft, all over. And he could not imagine a time when he didn't crave her. When his body didn't ache for her. "I have you."

And with that, he turned and walked out of the room.

Charity watched Rocco walk out, leaving her standing there with a hollow feeling in her stomach. Her legs began to shake, and she crumpled onto the floor, her dress billowing out around her.

She looked down at her hand, at the ring that Rocco had just presented her with. He had not put it on her finger. Of course, she hadn't allowed him to. But honestly, what good was it to have a man put a ring on your finger when you had to ask him to do it? He should have wanted to do it. In an ideal world he would've wanted to.

But this was not an ideal world. And their relationship wasn't real. Not to him.

She had to keep reminding herself that their relationship had started with a bag of lingerie and a threat. But it was so hard to remember that now, now when she felt so close to him. Now when she felt as if her next breath depended on having him with her.

The problem was she wanted more. She didn't want his ownership. She wanted his love. It felt nice at first, him saying she was his. Because no one had ever given her even that much. She had been a burden, not something anyone desired. But she was coming to realize that his wanting to possess her was not the same as him loving her.

And she wanted him to love her. She didn't want this desperate obsession, this compulsion he seemed to have to hang on to what he felt was his.

She wanted emotion. She wanted desire.

She had wanted to be loved all of her life, and she didn't want to spend the rest of it wishing for the same thing and getting nothing in return.

But she was trapped.

Unless she changed something.

Which was not going to happen while she sat here on her knees like someone in the throes of an emotional breakdown. Well, okay, so she kind of felt like someone in the throes of an emotional breakdown, but she wasn't helpless. And behaving like a helpless person was unacceptable.

She pushed herself up off the floor and adjusted her skirt, walking out of her bedroom and looking both ways down the corridor, searching for Rocco. She didn't know why, but she had the feeling he had gone to his room. He had never invited her into his room. It was one of his sacred spaces, and she was discovering he had a few of them.

Another bit of evidence that he didn't love her. There were too many parts of his life that he kept secret from her. That he kept only for himself.

Another thing that was about to end.

She walked down the hall, in the direction of his room, her teeth gritted in determination.

Thankfully, he did not have a keypad installed on his bedroom door. She turned the handle and pushed the door open, letting herself in with no announcement at all. Rocco was standing by his bed, undoing the cuffs on his shirt-sleeves. He lifted his head and turned to face her when she walked in, his expression fierce.

"What are you doing in here?"

"I didn't come to vacuum," she said, keeping her tone even.

He crossed his arms over his broad chest. "Speak."

"What if I told you I didn't want to get married?"

"I would tell you that's too damn bad." He dropped his arms back down at his sides. "Is that all?"

"I don't want to get married," she said, injecting as much steel into her voice as she could.

"Why are you telling me this now? While you're wearing your dress? It all looks a bit late for protesting, don't you think?"

Her heart burned in her chest, screaming at her to stop. Because she did want to get married. She wanted to marry him. She wanted to spend her life with him. But not under these circumstances. Not as a part of his plan for revenge, or possession, or restitution, or whatever this was. She wanted him to marry her because he wanted her. Because he loved her. Because he wanted to make a life with her.

"I don't think it's too late to protest until the marriage vows have been spoken." She took a deep breath. "With things as they are now, I don't want to marry you."

"You do not have a choice, *cara mia*," he said, lifting his hand and undoing the cuff that was still buttoned, rolling his shirtsleeves up to his elbows. "The decision has been made. And unless you want me to press charges…"

"So we're still at threats then, are we?"

"If that's what it takes."

"But I am your prisoner. Not your fiancée. I need you to understand that."

He reached out and grabbed hold of her wrist, lifting her hand in the air so that the light caught on the gem sparkling on her finger. "This suggests otherwise."

"But a fiancée can leave whenever she wants without the threat of jail time hanging over her head. A prisoner cannot. Don't lie to yourself, Rocco. Don't pretend this is something it isn't. Things haven't changed. On your end, they haven't changed. They are exactly the same as they've been from the beginning. You making demands, making threats if I don't comply with them. Even though I want you, it's always going to be colored by that. It's always going to be colored by the fact that I don't have another choice. So I'm telling you now, I do not want to be your wife."

He tugged her forward, lowering his head and kissing her, deep, hard. And she kissed him back, pouring every ounce of emotion into the kiss, her anger, her love, letting him have it all. And everything she gave, he took.

When they parted, they were both breathing hard. "It does not matter what you want. You will be my wife. That is final. Now, get out of my room and do not return here unless you're given an invitation."

Charity swallowed the lump made of grief and misery that was rising in her throat. "Okay. As long as we have an understanding."

"You are the only one who needs to understand."

She nodded once, and then turned and left him alone in his room. A wave of sadness, combined with an intense feeling of finality stole over her. And she had no idea what she felt at all. Because she wanted to be with him, and she had accomplished that.

But she wanted him to feel differently. And she couldn't force him to.

She was starting to think that a life with Rocco, with his emotions firmly cut off from her, would be much lonelier than a life without him.

But she would never find out. Because she did not have a choice. Or rather, she did. She could leave and test him, make him prove that he would send her to prison. But as much as she believed he wouldn't…could she risk it? She was guilty, and there was no denying it.

And if she were in prison what would it mean for her baby?

She couldn't leave, she wouldn't. But she wanted him to be certain of what he was doing.

What she had said to Rocco was true. He didn't really want a wife. He wanted a prisoner.

And he seemed intent on her serving a life sentence.

CHAPTER TEN

I DON'T WANT to be your wife.

Charity's words rang in his head as he stalked to his gallery, pain twisting his stomach like a knife stabbing him deep, sharp, deadly. He needed to be surrounded by his things.

He didn't know why she was suddenly fighting against him. Why she was making him feel as if he was a prison guard, keeping her in a leg shackle, when she had been treating him like a lover for the past few weeks. When she knew as well as he did that she responded to his every touch, his every kiss. He was not her enemy.

He had given her a ring. He had promised her his fidelity.

And this was how she repaid him, by standing there in the dress that he was buying for her and telling him she did not want to marry him.

She was *his*. She was his and there would be no negotiation on that score.

He turned and his eyes locked onto the army men that were on display in the corner of the room. It was a childish thing, he supposed, to keep those here among all of this priceless artwork. But he had liked the idea of having them. Of having something of his childhood returned to him.

The army men had been a gift from his mother, though not these exact toys, but toys just like them. Even after he had lost them, he had remembered them. Remembered the moment his mother had given them to him.

He gritted his teeth against the painful memories, memories it seemed were very close to the surface these days, and he couldn't quite fathom why. Memories of that horrible emptiness, of loss.

It made no sense. Charity was here, as secure as all of the things in this room. She couldn't leave him.

So why did it feel as though he had lost her?

Because you can't own a person. They have to choose you.

He didn't know where those words came from. He didn't know why this moment was blurring, images from the past intruding, taking over.

No one had chosen him. He had gone from family to family, each one keeping him for a set amount of time out of obligation, to collect their stipend from the government for taking part in the foster care system. But no one had chosen him.

He had aged out of the system without ever once having someone express interest in keeping him forever. Plenty of people had had legal claim over him during his growing-up years, but no one had chosen to keep him.

Mama chose you. Even though it cost her pride, her wealth, all the luxury she'd grown accustomed to. Her life.

He covered his eyes with his palms, digging the heels of his hands in hard. Trying to ease the ache that had taken up residence in his head.

What was the difference between those two things? He felt as if he was so close to it, so close that he could almost grasp hold of it. But it was hard, hard when he had spent so many years trying not to feel things. When he had spent so many years pretending emotions didn't matter.

Love.

No. His entire body rejected that. Because love was so painful. Love was devastating.

You couldn't buy it. You couldn't make it stay with you. You couldn't replace it.

But the effect of the gift remains...

He growled, turning back to the glass display case that contained the green plastic figures. It had never been about them. But about what he'd felt when she'd given them to him. About trying to recapture that, when he'd known he could never recapture her.

It was never about the *things*.

The emptiness was never about the loss of the toys.

But it would be so much easier if it were. Because he could buy things. He could replace things. But he could never replace the love that he'd had for the first five years of his life, and never again.

You can't make Charity love you by forcing her to stay with you.

The empty chamber inside his chest echoed now, pain radiating through his entire body. Because he knew it was true.

These things in this room had never given him anything. They were nothing but dead artifacts. Void of power, void of life. He had told himself that they would fix things, that they would make the emptiness go away. He had thought that by filling his house he would move farther and farther away from that small boy he had been, standing there in an empty hovel in Rome.

But all they had done was mask the loss.

He couldn't replace his mother with art, with cars, with money.

And he couldn't make Charity love him by forcing her to stay with him. She was right; she would never be anything but a prisoner as long as he made her stay.

You have to let her walk away. You have to give her the choice.

Everything inside of him rebelled against that. He wanted to lock her up. He wanted to keep her in this room, this room that was kept shut and secure with a code that only he knew.

But then everything between them would be empty. None of it would be real.

None of it was real at all until she made the choice.

She might say no.

He ignored that voice and walked out of the room, into the corridor. Yes, she might say no. But he had never given her the chance to say yes. And if she said yes...

He needed her to say yes.

He walked down the stairs and prowled through the main part of the house, unsure as to where he might find Charity. She had been avoiding him since their confrontation after the dress fitting, but only because he had been allowing it. He was not allowing it anymore.

And you are back to behaving as though you own her.

He gritted his teeth. Old habits die hard, especially when he didn't want to break them. But he had to. Because this was not about him anymore. It was about her.

He looked out onto the terrace and saw her standing there, her elbows rested on the balustrade. She was wearing a short, bright blue dress, her dark curls blowing in the breeze. She had never looked more beautiful. He had never felt a greater sense of her importance in his life.

And he was about to offer her freedom.

He was a fool.

He strode through the living area and out onto the terrace. "I will not send you to prison," he said, the words coming out clipped, rushed.

Charity looked up, whirling around to face him. She said nothing, her lips parted slightly, her brows raised.

"You are free. What I mean is you are free from any threat I have made to you. I will not press charges against you for the con you and your father ran. I do not care if he returns the money or not. You don't have to marry me. We will work out a custody deal with the child. I will pay child support. We will work out visitation. You have nothing to fear from me."

"You're letting me go?"

"Yes. I am letting you go." He swallowed hard, heavy, leaden weight settling deep in his chest. "You have nothing to fear from me."

"I don't have to stay?"

The way that she said it, the words she had chosen hit him with brutal force. "Of course you do not have to stay."

And he realized then that her answer was no. She didn't want to stay with him. And why would she? He had strong-armed her into this from the very beginning. Had made sure she knew that the only alternative to him was a jail cell. Why would she want him? He was a monster.

He had gone into all of this feeling as though he were the victim and she the criminal.

But he could not see it that way now.

"I thought you wanted to get married?"

"I do."

"Then why do you want to marry me?" she asked.

"Because," he said, his voice hard. "I am a possessive bastard. I don't want anyone else to have you."

"Is that all?"

Pain roared through his chest, a sharp tearing sensation rending through his heart. No, of course that wasn't all. But he didn't know what else there was. He didn't know how to say it. All he knew was that his head was pounding with pain, and that great, suffocating terror was gnawing at his throat. It all felt like trying to use a limb that was broken, mangled beyond repair. He knew in so many ways what he should do, what he should say, but he didn't have the strength.

Didn't have the strength to want something so fiercely again and be denied it.

And so he gave the only answer he could.

"There is nothing else."

She nodded slowly. "Okay. I'm going to pack my things. And I need for you to arrange for me to return to New York."

"That's it?"

"Yes," she said, her voice strangled. "If that's all you can say to me."

"I can't give you anything more," he said, hating himself because it was a lie. Hating himself because what it came down to was that he was simply too afraid to give anything more. And yet, he didn't know how to fight it. He didn't know how to be stronger.

Because everything that was rising up inside of him felt bigger than he was. Stronger. It was like a great, angry beast that had been kept locked down so deep he hadn't even realized it was there. And now that it had woken up it was starving, enraged and incapable of being satisfied. And he didn't want to try and satisfy it. He just wanted it to go away. Wanted the numbness he had felt for so many years to return.

And yet, right now he feared that would be impossible.

"Goodbye, Rocco. Please do get in touch about the custody arrangement."

"I will be there when you give birth," he said.

She nodded silently. "Okay."

"Is this it then?" It seemed wrong. It was far too quiet

an ending for something that had begun with so much fire. Yes, it had been a fire born of anger, but there had been passion, too. It'd been more than he had felt in years. And now it was simply ending. A dying flame, not ended dramatically with torrential downpours and wind, but with a slow and final suffocation.

"There was never really anything to end. Just a little bit of blackmail, right?"

"I suppose so." No. It had never only been blackmail. Not from the moment he'd first laid eyes on her. From that very moment it had been bigger than that, bigger than him.

And still he couldn't say it.

He felt like a little boy again, strangled by grief, strangled by fear, unable to speak the words that he so desperately needed to say.

"Then we'll be in touch."

"Yes, I daresay we will."

And so he stood there, as immovable as stone, his expression set, his jaw firmly clenched, while he screamed inside and watched Charity walk out of his life.

Charity managed to keep from breaking down until she was safely ensconced in Rocco's private plane.

But as soon as the doors to the aircraft closed and she looked around the empty cabin a sob escaped her lips, and tears started falling down her cheeks. She didn't want to leave. That was the worst part. She wanted to stay and accept whatever he was willing to give. Even though it wasn't what she wanted. Right now, she was wishing that she had decided to stay and take his crumbs, even though she needed more.

Because anything had to hurt less than this. A lifetime of knowing she was part of his collection, and only a possession to him, had to be better than a life without him. A life of knowing that he was sleeping with other women. That she would never fall asleep in his arms again. That he would never kiss her again.

They weren't going to be a family. That little part of herself that had—for the first time in years—let herself dream, felt like it was dying.

Unless he comes after you.

He could. He could still come after her. He wouldn't let her leave. Not after everything that had passed between them. Not after he had held her so close and told her she belonged to him. She had seen the way he kept his things, so secure, so safe. If she were one of his things, there was no way he would let her go.

He would come after her.

She waited while the minimal crew prepared the cabin for departure. Waited while the engine began to hum. And her tears fell harder, faster. And she realized that he was not going to come after her.

He can't.

And suddenly, she realized. Realized that she was an idiot. Realized what he was doing.

He was letting her go because he didn't see her as a possession. Not anymore.

He might not love her. He might never love her. She hated to think of that. Hated to face it. He was changing. This was a step for him. So far from the man who had sent that lingerie, that note, that demand. And that mattered.

She didn't want to be in love alone. But this was a test of that love, and she was failing it.

Love wasn't supposed to be this selfish.

No, her life hadn't been easy. But neither had Rocco's. She was learning, she was changing, and she was doing it faster than he was. But he had a harder climb. And if she wasn't standing at the top of the mountain waiting for him when he got there, then what good was her love?

It wasn't any better than the fickle parental love her father had often said he felt for her. He had only given it when it had suited him. And then, he had left her easily. Left her when she needed him most.

As she was doing to Rocco.

She was stronger than this. She wasn't going to run away like a coward when it got hard, when it got painful. She was going to fight. She was going to make demands, because damn it all, she was worth it.

She had spent all of her life waiting for someone to love her, but she had never once asked for love.

And now she wasn't just going to ask for it. She was going to demand it.

"Stop the plane." She realized that the staff couldn't hear her over the roar of the engine. "Stop the plane!"

Rocco had closed himself in his personal museum when Charity had gone off to pack.

He had been standing here, counting everything, taking mental inventory of everything for the past few hours. Everything was present. Nothing was missing. And yet his house felt empty. His body felt empty. As though Charity had torn something essential out of him and taken it away with her.

And none of these things helped. They didn't fill the emptiness.

Because you love her. And you were too much of a coward to say it.

The realization sent a searing bite of pain through his body. Yes, he did love her. But love was the most terrifying thing he could think of. Something he'd had for a mere five years before it had been torn from his life.

But the gift remains.

He pushed his hands through his hair, walking across the room and over to the display that held one of his vases. And then he pushed over the column that held it up, smashing both the glass case and the vase itself. He didn't feel any worse.

He turned and knocked over another display case, shattering the figurine that was beneath it. That was two things gone from his collection, and he didn't give a damn. Nothing mattered. None of it mattered.

These things that he had been protecting so jealously for so long, meant nothing. They offered no protection, no security. He was exposed. He was raw and wounded. And none of these *things* stopped the pain from roaring through him, savaging him.

She was all that mattered, and he had let her go.

She didn't choose you. You had to let her choose.

There was no reward in being virtuous. He laughed, the sound hollow, echoing in the room. He had spent so much of his life being decidedly unvirtuous because he had always known that there was no point to it. And truly, he had just now confirmed it.

He had done the right thing. And he felt no better for it. He certainly didn't feel enriched.

Now he would see his child whenever he was in New York. And what if she married someone else? Another man would be playing the part of father, living in the same household as his son or daughter. Another man would be sleeping with his woman.

Because whether or not he had let her go, he could not get rid of the feeling that she was his.

Always.

She might be gone, but the changes she'd made in him would stay.

He looked at the fractured glass on the floor, glittering against the marble. Those vases really didn't matter. These things didn't matter. He didn't need them.

That was new. It was different. It was because of her.

And no, he wouldn't have Charity. At least not now. But he would be a good father to his child. And without her, without having her in his life, he would not have been able to. Only a couple of months ago he had been prepared to never see the child. And now, that was unthinkable.

Yes, he had changed.

Though he certainly didn't feel very rewarded for it now, he knew he would be in the future. If for no other reason than that he would be able to have a relationship with his child. It was his chance to have love.

He walked across the broken glass, the pieces grinding beneath his shoes as he did so. He opened the doors and walked out into the main part of the house, then went up the stairs. He needed to shower. He needed to clear his mind. Figure out where to go from here.

He paused when he walked into his room and saw a bag sitting in the center of the bed.

He moved toward it, his heart pounding heavily. No one came in his room except for his staff. And even then, it was only when they were scheduled to be here. And no one was scheduled to be here now.

There was tissue paper in the top of the bag, and nestled in between the folds was an envelope. He picked it up, opened the flap and took out the note that was inside.

You will meet me on the terrace. In this bag you will find my engagement ring. If you have any interest in going forward with the wedding you will put this ring on my finger. And you will get down on one knee. There is no other option.

—C

With trembling fingers he took the tissue paper out of the bag and revealed the ring box sitting in the bottom. He picked it up, opened it. Inside was her ring. And she was here. She wasn't gone. She was on the terrace waiting for him.

He wrapped his fingers around the box, squeezing it tight in his palm as he walked out of the room and hurried down the stairs. When he reached the living area he froze. She was there, out on the terrace. She was there just as she had said she would be.

And he wasn't empty anymore.

She had *chosen* him.

He had to will himself to step forward. He was never nervous. He was always decisive. And yet, in this moment he found he was nervous. Still decisive. But nervous. Charity had the ability to turn his life upside down. Now and always.

He stopped in the doorway, taking a moment to admire her beauty. Taking a moment to relish her presence. He would never take it for granted. Never after this.

"You came back."

She lifted her head, a smile on her lips. "I didn't get very far. They started the engine of the plane and I started screaming and telling them to stop. I think they were concerned I was having some kind of medical episode."

"But you weren't."

"No. I just realized I was making a mistake."

He tightened his hold on the ring box. "Why? You seemed very sure when you left."

"I was waiting for something. But I hadn't given you

anything. I wanted you to give me a reason to stay, but I hadn't given you a reason to ask. I'm going to give you one now." She met his gaze, her eyes bright, fierce and wonderful. "I love you. And I do want to be your wife. What I didn't want was to be married to you only to have you ignore me, only to have you treat me like I'm simply a possession you can lock away for safekeeping. But I didn't even give you a chance. And I never told you. I never asked you to love me. So I'm telling you now. I'm asking you now. Because if I don't give you a chance, well…what kind of love is that?"

His heart beat faster, each thump painful, shocking. Had she truly said she loved him? Did she love him? "More than I deserve. I didn't give you a reason to give me a chance."

"Yes, you did. Things didn't start out very good between us. But you've changed. I've changed."

"I *have* changed. You have no idea how much."

"I do."

"No, you don't. Because I haven't told you everything. I haven't told you how I feel." He took a deep breath. "Charity, I love you. I should have told you earlier. But the very idea of love… It terrified me. Because I loved my mother, and I lost her. And I spent almost thirty years without love in my life. Sometime during my time being passed around foster homes I just decided I wouldn't need it anymore. But in order to force yourself into a place where you don't think you need love you have to forget what it feels like. You have to forget why it's good. In order to escape the bad emotions you have to turn off a lot of good ones, too. That was what I did. Until you."

"Rocco…"

"No, let me finish." He drew an unsteady breath. "There was a void in me. A void in my life. There has been ever since I lost my mother. And it was so much easier to pretend that the things, the house, all of those material items were a part of that void. Because they were replaceable. And so I pretended that my money, that my collections were taking steps and fixing that, but they were only masking the real problem. That there was no love in my life, in me. But my mother sacrificed everything to take care of me. To raise me for as long as she did. I forgot that sacrifice. I forgot the importance of her love because it was too painful. And I became something... Something she would not have been proud of. But I want to change that. I want to be a good father to our child. I want to be a good husband to you. I want to stop being afraid. Because I don't think love and fear can exist in the same heart."

"Rocco, I love you, too," she said, closing the distance between them and kissing his lips. The most profound sense of relief, of peace washed over him. Happiness. Such a strange thing to feel happy after so many years of pretending it didn't matter.

"Such a strange thing, Charity. You are in so many ways my very worst nightmare. You stole my money from me, and you know what an offense that was to a man like me. Then, you stole my heart. The thing I protected above everything else. And yet, I am so grateful you did."

"Yes, well I am sorry about the money. Less so about your heart."

"I'm not sorry about either one. Seeing as it brought us together."

"What are we going to do when our child asks how we met?"

He laughed, and for the first time in a long time, there was humor in the sound. "We tell him the truth I suppose. That I met a beautiful thief and whisked her away to my private island where we fell in love. He will not believe us, naturally. Which is why, in this case, I believe the truth will serve us well."

"When you put it like that it all sounds very romantic."

"Is it not? I was under the impression it was." He opened his hand and looked down at the ring box in his palm. "At least, it will be if the rest of this goes well." He sank down to his knee in front of her, and he found it was the most natural thing in the world. "Will you give me your hand?"

"Of course," she said, her voice thick with tears.

He took her left hand in his, and this time, he placed the ring on her finger. "Charity, will you marry me?"

"Yes," she said.

Finally, she had said yes to him.

Finally, she had chosen him.

He stood and pulled her into his arms, kissing her deeply, fiercely. "I love you," he said. "And I will be a terrible husband. At least at first. Because I am changing, but you know it has been slow. I will make mistakes. It's going to take me some time to understand all of these new feelings. But I want to. Because you are more important than protecting myself. And you are certainly more important than my pride. Than anything in my collection. I broke a vase."

Her dark eyes went wide. "You didn't."

"I did. I broke two of them."

"Rocco, why would you do that?"

"Because I was angry. And because they didn't matter. The only thing that mattered was you. And you are not a thing. I cannot collect you. I cannot own you. And the truth of the matter is I don't want to. Because I like it when you fight me, I like it when you disagree with me. I like your mind as well as your body. I don't want to subject you—I want you to stand equal with me. I don't want to change your life more than you've changed mine."

"Before I met you I didn't feel like I knew myself. I felt like each and every thing I did was just another role I was playing. I felt so thin…so insubstantial. But you looked at me and you told me I was priceless. You told me I mattered. When everyone else made me feel like I made their life less…you made me feel like that couldn't be true. Not if I was worth so much in your eyes. And I know who I am now. And I know what I want. More than that…I know what I deserve."

"And what is that, *cara mia*?"

"To be loved. And to have you. I want you."

"Anything else?" he asked, kissing her again.

She waved her hand. "Oh, there's a whole list of things. But we can sort that out later."

"Can we?"

She fluttered her lashes at him. "I want a pony."

He chuckled. "We'll discuss it," he said.

"Why don't we discuss it after we go upstairs for a while? I have a feeling you'll be in a better mood by then."

"I have been in a better mood since the moment you walked into my life."

"Really?"

"Well, not every moment of it."

She smiled. "Good. I would hate to become predictable."

"Now that is one thing I think we will never have to worry about."

"Yeah, a reformed con woman married to an Italian billionaire. One thing is certain—our lives will never be boring."

EPILOGUE

CHARITY WAS RIGHT about that. She was right about a great many things over the next fifteen years, but the fact that their lives wouldn't be boring was chief among them. It was impossible to be bored with four children.

Even more impossible now that they were all either teenagers, or edging into their teenage years. No one could say that their household was lacking in drama.

In fact, there was a healthy amount of drama happening about ten feet down the coast from where she and Rocco were currently standing.

Lilia, their oldest, was currently being tormented by Marco, the youngest, and a piece of seaweed, while the middle two, Analise and Lucia, looked on in a state of amusement.

Charity glanced over at her husband, who appeared as amused as the children. "You should stop him," she said.

"Probably," Rocco said, turning and smiling at her.

That smile never failed to make her knees weak. Still. After all this time.

"You aren't going to."

"I didn't have siblings, but I like to think that if I did I would have done things very similar to the way Marco does them. He's a smart boy. The only boy, so he must make the most of that."

"He's a handful."

"I think he gets it from you, actually."

Charity laughed. "You think I'm a handful?"

Rocco leaned in and kissed her neck, and a shiver went through her body. "You do fit my hands perfectly."

It was funny now to think back on how they had met. To think about finding out she was pregnant with Lilia. How terrified she had been. How angry she had been when Rocco had insisted he be a part of the child's life.

If she had only had a window into how things would be in the future, she never would have hesitated.

She could remember clearly that moment when she had told Rocco about the baby, and when she had left his office. How, even in her misery, she had thought that at least she had the possibility of a new start.

She had been right about that at least. She just hadn't been right about the details.

She could never have fathomed this much happiness. Could never have imagined that her life would be so full of love.

She had gone twenty-two years feeling as if no one loved her. And in the fifteen years since she had met Rocco she had never gone a day without feeling loved. Without *knowing* she was loved. She never felt as if she was standing on the outside. She was wrapped in it.

"You know, I'm very glad I stole your money," she said.

He tilted his head to the side. "What brought that on?"

"I was just thinking about how we met. How you changed my life."

"Well, I'm very glad I caught you."

"I'm glad you caught me, too."

"More than that, I'm glad you decided to stay caught."

"Me, too."

"You know, as much as I don't like to think about what

an ass I was back when we first met, I was thinking the other day about what I said to you in the hotel that first day."

"Were you?"

"Yes," he said, his tone grave. "I told you that you got the better end of the deal. Seeing as I had spent a million dollars on sex."

She rolled her eyes. "Oh yes, how could I forget?"

"You can't. I was horrible. But, I was thinking now, knowing what I do, I should have given you everything then and there."

"Because having a wife and children has proven to be so expensive?" she asked, smiling broadly.

"No, because you are priceless. I know that now with a depth of certainty that surpasses all else. Years of watching you, growing with you, loving you, have only strengthened my love. And I would give everything, then and now, to have you in my life forever." He cupped her cheek, bending down and kissing her on the lips. "All I have is worth nothing if I don't have you."

She looked up at her husband, warmth, love, flooding through her. "You have me. Forever."

* * * * *

Available July 21, 2015

#3353 CHATSFIELD'S ULTIMATE ACQUISITION
The Chatsfield
by Melanie Milburne

Isabelle Harrington is *furious* when arrogant playboy Spencer Chatsfield becomes her new boss. He's also the man who shattered her heart years ago. The only thing she can't stand more than Spencer is the sizzling chemistry *still* burning between them!

#3354 THE GREEK DEMANDS HIS HEIR
The Notorious Greeks
by Lynne Graham

Leo Zikos is pleased to have secured a perfectly *convenient* fiancée, until Grace Donovan's impeccable beauty tempts him to pursue one last night of freedom... But that night, and the positive pregnancy test that follows, blows Leo's plans apart!

#3355 HIS SICILIAN CINDERELLA
Playboys of Sicily
by Carol Marinelli

Matteo Santini bought one night with Bella Gatti to protect her innocence, but then she disappeared. Now, forced together at a wedding, he wants a reckoning. The only way Bella will be leaving the party is with Matteo—via his bed!

#3356 THE PERFECT CAZORLA WIFE
by Michelle Smart

Charley Cazorla strides back into her soon-to-be ex-husband's life with a plan. Except Raul has his own ideas! To save Charley's business, the Spaniard demands his own payment: she must resume her role as the *perfect* wife—in *every* sense!

#3357 THE SINNER'S MARRIAGE REDEMPTION
Seven Sexy Sins
by Annie West

Flynn Marshall is determined to rush stunning Ava Cavendish to the altar at the first opportunity. A trophy bride should complete his plans, but the desire Ava inflames in this untouchable CEO soon turns his ordered strategy on its head...

#3358 THE MARAKAIOS BABY
The Marakaios Brides
by Kate Hewitt

Margo Ferras knows that she must give up devilishly seductive Leo Marakaios in order to protect her heart. But when she discovers that she's pregnant with his child, Margo walks back into Leo's life and asks *him* to marry *her*!

#3359 CAPTIVATED BY THE GREEK
by Julia James

Salesgirl Mel may not be Nikos Parakis's type, but she can't resist his tempting offer: a no-strings romance under the sizzling sun. But parting ways is made impossible when sultry nights with the captivating Greek leave Mel carrying his heir!

#3360 CLAIMED FOR HIS DUTY
Greek Tycoons Tamed
by Tara Pammi

Stavros Sporades agreed to marry heiress Leah Huntington to protect her, but now she's demanding a divorce! Stavros wants proof Leah's troubled past is behind her, but one night of desire reveals that she might have been innocent all along...

YOU CAN FIND MORE INFORMATION ON UPCOMING HARLEQUIN® TITLES, FREE EXCERPTS AND MORE AT WWW.HARLEQUIN.COM.

HPCNM0715RB

REQUEST YOUR FREE BOOKS!

HARLEQUIN

Presents®

2 FREE NOVELS PLUS
2 FREE GIFTS!

PASSION GUARANTEED SEDUCTION

YES! Please send me 2 FREE Harlequin Presents® novels and my 2 FREE gifts (gifts are worth about $10). After receiving them, if I don't wish to receive any more books, I can return the shipping statement marked "cancel." If I don't cancel, I will receive 6 brand-new novels every month and be billed just $4.30 per book in the U.S. or $5.24 per book in Canada. That's a saving of at least 13% off the cover price! It's quite a bargain! Shipping and handling is just 50¢ per book in the U.S. and 75¢ per book in Canada.* I understand that accepting the 2 free books and gifts places me under no obligation to buy anything. I can always return a shipment and cancel at any time. Even if I never buy another book, the two free books and gifts are mine to keep forever.

106/306 HDN GHRP

Name	(PLEASE PRINT)	
Address		Apt. #
City	State/Prov.	Zip/Postal Code

Signature (if under 18, a parent or guardian must sign)

Mail to the **Reader Service**:
IN U.S.A.: P.O. Box 1867, Buffalo, NY 14240-1867
IN CANADA: P.O. Box 609, Fort Erie, Ontario L2A 5X3

**Are you a current subscriber to Harlequin Presents® books
and want to receive the larger-print edition?
Call 1-800-873-8635 or visit www.ReaderService.com.**

* Terms and prices subject to change without notice. Prices do not include applicable taxes. Sales tax applicable in N.Y. Canadian residents will be charged applicable taxes. Offer not valid in Quebec. This offer is limited to one order per household. Not valid for current subscribers to Harlequin Presents books. All orders subject to credit approval. Credit or debit balances in a customer's account(s) may be offset by any other outstanding balance owed by or to the customer. Please allow 4 to 6 weeks for delivery. Offer available while quantities last.

Your Privacy—The Reader Service is committed to protecting your privacy. Our Privacy Policy is available online at www.ReaderService.com or upon request from the Reader Service.

We make a portion of our mailing list available to reputable third parties that offer products we believe may interest you. If you prefer that we not exchange your name with third parties, or if you wish to clarify or modify your communication preferences, please visit us at www.ReaderService.com/consumerschoice or write to us at Reader Service Preference Service, P.O. Box 9062, Buffalo, NY 14240-9062. Include your complete name and address.

HP15

SPECIAL EXCERPT FROM

 HARLEQUIN

Presents

Does Charley Cazorla dare return to her husband's bed? Does she even have a choice, when Raul is offering a deal she really can't refuse...?

Read on for an exclusive excerpt of this stunning new book by **Michelle Smart**
THE PERFECT CAZORLA WIFE

"It won't happen again," she promised through ragged breaths.

"I think you've told enough lies this past week, don't you?"

Raul sat back down, waiting for the thunder beneath his rib cage to abate.

How had things gotten out of hand so quickly?

He'd been taunting her, teasing her, asserting his control, spelling out to her how much he held the upper hand. He'd enjoyed it but had kept his mind firmly on the seduction in hand.

She'd been the one to kiss him, a fact that, from the look on her face, she regretted hugely.

She'd hooked her arm around his neck and his mind had gone blank, desire overshadowing everything else.

The chemistry between them had always been explosive, but that...

It had felt as if a coil locked in a too-tight box had finally sprung free.

He'd been seconds away from taking her on the table.

She still stood there, her green eyes firing their hatred at him.

Whom did she hate the most? Him for compelling her back into his bed? Or herself for wanting it?

"So, *cariño*, do we have a deal?" He was gratified to hear his voice functioning as normal. He would *never* allow himself to show weakness in front of her. "The day care centre, signed, sealed, delivered and renovated in exchange for four months in my bed?"

Four months. That would surely be enough to get her out of his system once and for all.

Maybe it was fortuitous that she'd walked back into his life at this moment. He needed to move on, not just from the dissolution of their marriage but from the sexual hold she still held over him.

Her chin rose, her pretty nostrils flaring. "Yes. I accept your terms, but with one condition of my own—I won't be sharing your bed until the deeds of the building are in my hands."

"The building will be in the Cazorla name by the end of the week."

"Then you'll have to wait until then before you can touch me again."

"You are not in a position to make any demands, *cariño*."

Don't miss
THE PERFECT CAZORLA WIFE *by Michelle Smart,*
available August 2015 wherever
Harlequin Presents® books and ebooks are sold.

www.Harlequin.com

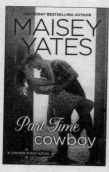 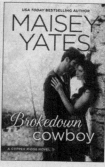 

HARLEQUIN

Presents®

A stunning conclusion to Carol Marinelli's latest
duet, *Playboys of Sicily*, packed full of fiery passion,
dangerous temptation and heart-stopping excitement!

His until midnight…?

Losing her virginity to millionaire Matteo Santini came
at a high price for chambermaid Bella—unable to leave
Sicily with Matteo the next day, she lost her heart *and*
her one chance at happiness that night…

But now Matteo's back and more irresistible than ever!
Thrown together at Sicily's most exclusive wedding,
their sizzling attraction still burns bright, and as the
clock strikes midnight, it's clear the only way Bella will
be leaving the party is with Matteo—via his bed!

Find out what happens next in:

HIS SICILIAN CINDERELLA
AUGUST 2015

Stay Connected:

www.Harlequin.com

www.IHeartPresents.com

f /HarlequinBooks

🐦 @HarlequinBooks

📌 /HarlequinBooks

HP13361